NICKY ANT____

Marie-Cla

Mad Shadows

Translated from the French by
Merloyd Lawrence

Introduction: Naim Kattan
General Editor: Malcolm Ross
New Canadian Library No. 78

M&S

Canadian Cataloguing in Publication Data

Blais, Marie-Claire, 1939 –
[La belle bête. English]
Mad shadows

(New Canadian library ; N78)
Translation of: La belle bête.
ISBN 0-7710-9178-8

I. Title. II. Title: La belle bête. English
III. Series: New Canadian library ; no. 78.

PS8503.L35B4413 1987   C843'.54   C87-095127-0
PQ3919.2.B53B4413 1987

Manufactured in Canada by Webcom Limited

McClelland and Stewart
The Canadian Publishers
481 University Avenue
Toronto, Ontario
M5G 2E9

CONTENTS

Introduction

When *Mad Shadows* (or *La belle bête*, as it was called in French), was first published in 1959, it caused considerable astonishment. What particularly captured public attention was the phenomenon of a twenty-year-old girl being capable of making such a flamboyant entrance into literature. This, of course, was during the period when the enormous success of Françoise Sagan had stimulated certain critics, and especially certain publishers, to find – or create – her sisters. As a result, twenty-year-old girls in Japan, Israel, Lebanon, England, and the United States were cynically proclaiming their non-conformity and recounting sexual adventures which their mothers, at the same age, would have blushed to hear.

As a natural consequence of this situation, Marie-Claire Blais was treated as a prodigy and therefore isolated at the very outset of her career. But as new books followed one another at a dizzying rate, their scope and variety made it increasingly difficult for the critics to categorize her and they were obliged to modify their analyses and interpretations. Not a year has gone by without a play, a collection of poems, or a novel by Marie-Claire Blais, and her work has very quickly found an international audience. In the beginning this acclaim was mainly due to the interest shown in her by the American writer, Edmund Wilson, who even pronounced her a genius. Her books were translated into English and brought out in the United States and Canada. Publication in France followed, and in 1966 she was awarded one of the prestigious French literary prizes, the Prix Médicis, for her novel *A Season in the Life of Emmanuel*. American and French criticism added weight to the confusion and misinterpretation which, even today, still surround her work. From the time of Wilson's early assessment, her novels have been considered as brilliant descriptions of a French Canadian society, freeing itself slowly and painfully from the throes of a rigorous and retrograde Catholicism. It has been very interesting to read certain Canadian critics, and particularly to see the reaction of those readers who felt that *A Season in the Life of Emmanuel* was a vicious, morbid, and false description of those aspects of French Canadian society against which the young writer was revolting. One misunderstanding led to another and Marie-Claire Blais finally found herself defined as something between a highly singular novelty and a conventional realist.

More than ten years have passed since the publication of *Mad Shadows*, and it is now possible to give the book its proper position within the body of Marie-Claire Blais' subsequent work and also to read it in the perspective of the development of French Canadian writing during this period. Many of our early writers monotonously sang the praises of Quebec rural life and the essential role the Catholic church was playing in French Canada and in North America. Then a new generation of writers arose, whose view, if not actually neutral or detached, at least lacked religious and patriotic commitment – both Roger Lemelin and Gabrielle Roy are good examples of this position. But even then, such poets as Saint-Denys-Garneau, and later Anne Hébert, had already begun to reveal their uncertainty regarding the solidity of traditional values and to question the psychological and spiritual order of their society. Novelists like Robert Elie and André Langevin were soon to follow in their footsteps.

But it was Jean Le Moyne, in *Convergences*, who gave precise and explicit expression to the religious and psychological anxiety felt by many French Canadians. He was not satisfied with simply acknowledging his Christian faith. He also gave free rein to his religious fervour. And he openly challenged the Christian religion as lived by his people. To him, the dualism born of Jansenism and Puritanism was not an aspect of Christianity but ultimately its negation. Separation of flesh and spirit, body and soul, with all nobility being ascribed to soul and spirit, seemed to him to be a distortion of a religion that proclaims and establishes the unity of man. Rejection of the body, rejection of woman, is in the last analysis a rejection of the self.

It is now possible to see the two apparently contradictory ways in which, from her very first book, Marie-Claire Blais has grappled with the realities of the society of her birth. She denied these realities and, in order to accomplish this, treated them as a nightmare. Indeed it was only by exaggeration, by plunging as deeply as possible into the abyss, that she was able to achieve integration. Otherwise, she would have been unable to work. And writing, with her, springs from this need to reconstitute and restructure as myth the otherwise unendurable nightmare. Thus, once she has denied reality and by this means removed its power to destroy the individual, literature prompts her to dominate it by mythicizing it. Consequently, in her choice and use of material, there is a rejection of the real world and a deliberate construction of a second reality. To tell the nightmare is to free oneself from it, to escape its power. And the fantastic elements in the narration become a screen that obliterates reality and protects the creator. Through this screen nature loses its transparency, its concrete solidity. It fades into a mist. In *Mad Shadows*, when Marie-Claire Blais describes a lake or a farm or alludes to a train, we have the continuous impression that *that* lake, farm, or train is at once more or less than itself. It is more because it is endowed with a magic force which acts upon the humans who encounter it. It is less because it eludes one's grasp. The man who places himself outside, in order to objectively observe such things, or who simply integrates them into his everyday existence can never apprehend their varying dimensions. Nature, with Marie-Claire Blais, is ethereal, and volatile. It only recovers its immobility and firmness when, like a faithful mirror, it reflects the nebulous human beings who look into it. Patrice gazes at himself in the lake, but his face does not thereby acquire the expression it lacks. The characters in this novel cannot attach themselves to a natural world that has no weight.

Will their reality then, be the community that surrounds them and will other people give their existence an opacity? We soon begin to realize that each of the main characters in *Mad Shadows* is as isolated from society as from nature. True, Marie-Claire Blais mentions neighbours, refers to passengers on the train, or a party in the village, but she is only indicating, lightly and furtively, that the world of men does actually exist and surround the characters she is presenting.

But the family which composes the universe of the book, in order to protect itself from complete isolation and the menace of a fluid society and an intangible natural world, could have tightened its bonds and created its own microcosm. Its solitude would then have been collective and its isolation easier to bear.

vii

We discover quite quickly that this also is not within its scope.

If Patrice stares at himself in the lake, his narcissism is not exclusive to him. All the characters in the novel are enclosed in a prison of which they are quite conscious, but from which they cannot manage to escape. Patrice is enclosed in his idiocy. He is an incomplete human being, not yet in possession of his soul. He emerges slowly from heavy shadows of unawareness. He is beautiful, but even his beauty is insubstantial, brought alive only by his mother's admiration. Without her looking at him it remains abstract, dead. He will have many stages to pass through before he escapes from limbo.

Isabelle-Marie, his sister, is as stricken as he; and, like him, she was born diminished, she is ugly. And though she does not lack awareness, this cannot restore an equilibrium shattered at the outset by nature. Instead, it makes her condition unbearable. She, also, must pass through many stages – violence, malice, despair – before she overcomes the absence of all sense of unity in her existence.

The mother, Louise, is a person of unbounded egotism. Light-headed, she admires herself in the image reflected by her mirror and in that other image she has created – the face and body of her son. She loves Patrice because he is absent as a living person and present as an unmoving image. She creates her own idea of herself with the distance and detachment of a disinterested observer. She, too, attains awareness by encountering an increasing number of obstacles, each time losing a portion of her own entity: that unity of her personality which has no other foundation but her awareness. She experiences suffering, illness, and even alienation from herself before she finds death. Her lover, Lanz, is crippled and masks his ugliness and his physical decline with disguises. Revelation of the naked truth costs him his life. Isabelle-Marie's husband is blind. The awareness that comes to him with sight forces him away from his wife and daughter. The light is more blinding than night.

The five characters in this novel are all deformed. Louise is stupid, Isabelle-Marie ugly, Patrice an idiot, Lanz lame, and Michael blind. But physical deformity only expresses a more fundamental deformity, an essential flaw in the soul. No love binds them to one another. Earth evades them and God is so far away they do not even suspect His existence. They have not yet been born into life. They have not received grace. They have not been redeemed. They are victims, with no power to choose between good and evil since they do not possess free will. Not only were they born crippled but what they received as gratuitous gifts at birth is taken from them. Lanz loses his life; Louise loses her empty beauty when she is stricken by cancer of the face; and Patrice is disfigured. Evil exists and enters these lives without anyone's being able to explain why or how it came. The fate that strikes these beings is as blind as they are, and they are powerless to react. Their will to fight back was absent in them from the very beginning of their lives, when they were born deformed and crippled.

The novel can be read as a metaphor, a phantasmagoria of the world before birth, a universe in limbo, where God has not yet appeared, free will does not exist, and the limit has not been drawn between good and evil. Men are born and they are incomplete. They are spiritually stunted and only reach human stature at the cost of the numerous wounds that they inflict upon others and themselves. By suffering on the threshold of death, those that have survived the agonies of the crucified find their souls. The "beautiful beast" is transformed into a man. This is a religion of laceration. It is without grace, without charity, and without love. The only spiritual exercise granted to a man is suffering.

The Jansenism also is complete. Not only is there dichotomy – separation of soul and body – but atrophy of the soul in those individuals in whom it is not entirely absent. This is a universe that antecedes sin and that may herald life. It is inhabited by death. It is a nightmare that only the Word redeems.

By this primary and primordial grammar of the soul, Marie-Claire Blais marks her first steps on the road she was later to follow in her search for the existence of a genuine unity between flesh and spirit.

A few years later, another young French-Canadian writer, Réjean Ducharme, formulated his own grammar, but with him it was language that defined the soul. Identity was obtained by play upon words and stylistic brilliance. In *Mad Shadows* we can already see a body of work in germ, and the novel seems in retrospect to be the herald of all those that have come after it. In *A Season in the Life of Emmanuel, The Manuscripts of*

Pauline Archange, and the play, *The Execution*, once the children are born they are fated to grope their way painfully between the shadows of the death from which they are freeing themselves and the shadows of the sin that threatens them at every moment. They owe the rare, bright intervals in their lives to their own weak wills and the caprices of fate. They move between possible annihilation and necessary violence — incomplete beings who are wresting their identity slowly and with immense difficulty from a world in which twilight reigns. Marie-Claire Blais seems to draw these characters from the indefinite, the imprecise, the non-existent. They *are* at the instant of birth. They are also incomplete, deformed, fragile, and powerless against fate. They are not yet born. The world does not exist. This is a universe of phantoms and shadows, nightmares translated into words. We are on the threshold of life. Literature here becomes a herald, because it is a harbinger of the potential life which it is attempting to liberate.

Naim Kattan
Ottawa

(Translated by Joyce Marshall)

Descend the way that leads to hell infernal;
Plunge in a deep gulf where crime's inevitable,
Flagellated by a wind driven from the skies eternal,

Where all your torments, and for all the ages,
Mad shadows, never at the end of your desires,
Shall never satisfy your furious rages,
And your chastisement be born of loveless fires.

BAUDELAIRE,
Flowers of Evil

*
ONE

*

1

The
train
was
leaving
town.

Lying back with his head against his mother's shoulder, Patrice followed the dappled countryside with a melancholy expression. Behind his forehead everything grew confused, like a billowing stormcloud on a screen. He watched in silence and did not understand, but his idiot face was so dazzling that it made one think of genius. His mother caressed the nape of his neck with the palm of her hand. With a gentle slip of her all-too-supple wrist she could lower Patrice's head to her bosom and hear his breathing more easily.

On the other side, aloof and motionless, her daughter Isabelle-Marie sat pressing her sharp features against the window. Louise often said to herself, 'Isabelle-Marie never really had the face of a child . . . But Patrice . . . Oh, Patrice!'

Isabelle-Marie was thirteen. She was tall and emaciated; her alarming eyes, so often full of anger, seemed glued to black bone. When she scowled, the lower part of her face twisted into a look of fierce contempt. It was almost frightening.

Her mother Louise, who was rich and owned many farms, gave her daughter all the most menial chores in order to devote her life and her remaining youth to Patrice. One could see that Louise believed in herself and above all, to the point of obsession, in the beauty of Patrice.

In the seats nearby, the passengers were looking at her son. Weary of having nothing to think about, the child yielded to sleep, gently, with a drop of perspiration on his brow. Louise wiped the drop away with the tip of her finger and smiled with pride at the thought that the beauty of her son was becoming ever more devastating, to even the coldest onlooker.

'Patrice . . . such a magnificent child!'

At the same moment, Isabelle-Marie thought, Patrice, the Idiot!

Patrice did not seem to worry about himself. He pressed even closer to his mother, his large green eyes empty as the night. Now and then his eyelashes and his cheeks would tremble, suddenly, and not in unison. His forehead was white, intact, and soft as the thigh of a swan. His bare lips curved without the slightest trace of tension. Never was there a sign of life on these lips. The lips of a corpse. Isabelle-Marie cast a sly look at him.

'A Beautiful Beast!' she muttered between her teeth.

Louise did not question the intelligence of her ten-year-old Adonis. He spoke very little, but she attributed this speechlessness, like the silence of the gods, to unconcern.

His extraordinary beauty satisfied her every wish. Nevertheless, Patrice was an idiot. Isabelle-Marie knew that behind his pale forehead was the deep stupor of an inactive mind, the lethargy of a dead brain. How cold it must be beneath his skin, she thought and was ashamed to see him sleeping peacefully, protected by his mother's shoulder. She knew that the woman's eyes, indeed her whole being, rested on this solitary and fragile beauty.

16

The passengers never stopped looking at Patrice. Isabelle-Marie began to blush. She felt sick to her stomach. Soon she saw nothing outside the window. A strange desire to die came over her. She rose and pressed against the cold glass. Her bruised cheek shivered. In an awkward attempt to hide her trembling, Isabelle-Marie clawed at the pane with her nails, trying to hold onto it . . . Louise did not see her. Louise never really dared look at her. Finally Isabelle-Marie buried her face in her hands.

'Mother, I have a fever.'

Bewildered, physically terrified by the people around her, she heard a woman cry out, 'What a handsome son you have!'

And Louise, in her contented voice, answered, 'Isn't he, though?'

Isabelle-Marie fainted.

When she opened her eyes, they were drawing into the station. The other passengers, she was relieved to discover, had forgotten about the beauty of her brother. They walked hurriedly toward the station, paying no attention to one another. Isabelle-Marie began to breathe again. Blood warmed her legs and she felt a sense of release, a crazy desire to burst out laughing now that the torture had ceased.

'What is it, Isabelle-Marie?' asked Louise in a deceitful tone of voice.

'Nothing at all, Mother. Only a slight dizziness . . .'

Louise held her son's hand nested in her own and the two of them slipped through the crowd, oblivious of the smoke that filled the air. The blond child followed indolently, his head resting against his mother's elbow. Isabelle-Marie was sorry that the sun cast such an aura of innocence over Patrice's hair. She followed her brother, awkward in her black dress . . . and more awkward still in the flesh.

Convinced that Patrice had certain special gifts, Louise entrusted him to private tutors, but one by one they left, disappointed, aware of Patrice's stupidity and of his mother's grotesque illusion. Of course none of them would ever have been able to say, 'Madame, your son is an idiot,' or 'This child has no intelligence,' and with these few words to dampen Louise's great passion, a passion which had begun with the birth of this spoiled creature, this body made to house a nonexistent mind. Louise went right on glorifying her son, as though in a dream, supplying, when necessary, the soul which was lacking. If Patrice was silent, it was because he was savoring some secret insight. If Patrice repeated the same meaningless gestures in all his games, it was because he was guided by an instinctive sense of his own beauty. She was his slave. She lent him her own intelligence. She treated him as an exceptional being and carefully spared him from failure. Her child-god! And so the Beautiful Beast wanted nothing; it ate, slept, smiled, and laughed when it saw others laughing. The Beautiful Beast would soon be fifteen years old.

Devoting herself more and more to the needs of her son, Louise prepared him the most delicious meals, helped him in the care of his body, and introduced him to Vanity by placing him in front of mirrors though in this, as in everything else, Patrice showed great lethargy. She sated him with walks, with horseback riding. He took to horses immediately, out of instinct. Patrice was obedient. He cried when he was told to, responded to her tenderness without knowing why. He had never discovered anything, not even his mother's love, or Isabelle's jealousy.

He was destined to know nothing but his own beauty. This he discovered.

*

2

It was summertime. Isabelle-Marie worked in the fields, grimy with sweat, her hair across her cheeks, with callused fingers and a salty taste in her mouth. Ever since the beginning of the season she had felt a sharp ache in her chest. This ache drained her energy and her flesh clung to her bones like a hot shroud. Never had the sun been so strong; lethal and scorching, it tanned the farmers and dried up the earth. Isabelle-Marie's nerves were taut, exposed. In the evening when she returned to the huge deserted house, she found Patrice wallowing in a life of indolence, and Louise living by her whims. Exasperated, she swallowed her fury, her heart crying out for justice. But rebellion gave her strength and her hands grew sharp as knives.

One day, when Louise was in town, Isabelle-Marie took her brother for a swim. In spite of her appalling jealousy, she tried to feel a spark of sisterly affection. At the lake, she was able to forget about the scars that covered her back. When she swam, her limbs relaxed, one by one, and her body drank the bliss of adolescence. Was she capable of enjoying life, like Louise and Patrice? No. Crushed and humiliated for so long, Isabelle-Marie experienced pleasure as a kind of delirium, an emotion which consumed both flesh and blood: love of the earth, love in the face of ingratitude. As she surrendered her body to the cold water, she was almost happy to be so different from Patrice and Louise. She shook her head. The drops of water ran together, streaming down the side of her cheek.

Then she cried out, 'Patrice . . . are you coming, Patrice?'

Half-naked, resplendent, Patrice was kneeling. He seemed to be trying to disappear into the depths of the lake.

'Patrice, what are you doing there?'

He did not answer and remained motionless. Isabelle swam quietly in his direction. She could not help but admire him, and his beauty made her blush.

'Patrice . . .'

His back was curved in a graceful arc, exposing the tender, inviolate nape which Louise so loved to caress and which gleamed, fresh and childlike, as though just removed from its original mould.

He is contemplating himself! thought Isabelle-Marie.

Yes, Patrice was contemplating his own body, floating and yet perfectly balanced in the water.

'Patrice! Patrice!'

She shouted, hoping to frighten him.

But Patrice was not listening. Patrice was looking at himself, and for the first time his beauty meant something to him. Leaning over to look at his body, he trembled, feeling so contained, so handsome . . . The one quality which made him a man! Finally he raised his eyes, eternally confident in his own being. He began to walk in the sand, mysterious, virginal, his forehead glowing strangely. Isabelle-Marie fled, repelled. Patrice did not stop to notice the bird with one wing flying near him, nor the thin legs of his sister fluttering over the pebbles. He smiled; a warmth rose within him and his muscles cried out in triumph. From then on Patrice knew that he was beautiful, and beauty was to become the goal of his life. Patrice had become the god of Patrice. His soul was too feeble to ask for more.

'Patrice, my darling Patrice . . . Where have you been?'

He was sitting on the edge of his mother's bed, empty-handed, staring into space. Instinct brought him into Louise's room where everything somehow belonged to him, a room created for his ease and comfort. Louise would untangle his long hair, and her gestures were a way of enfolding him in tenderness. 'Now then, what did my baby do today?' she would ask. But he did not have to answer. Sometimes he could not remember what he had done. Louise asked other things: 'Don't you think the earth has a strange odor this year?' Then, with her head thrown back, as though over-whelmed by the weight of her hair, she would wander back and forth in the room, explaining new plans to develop her farms. Patrice would give dull nods of agreement, which delighted her.

This morning she asked him, 'You are sad . . . What are you thinking about?'

He smiled, shrugging his shoulders, and the smile that brightened his eyes dimmed the whiteness of his eyelids.

'I'm not thinking about anything, Mother.'

She laughed.

'Oh, come now, my darling boy isn't telling me the truth.'

But he was telling the truth.

He let his mother kiss him on the forehead, wished her good morning, and then left the room.

After walking around the garden for several hours, he stopped to listen . . . His sister was sobbing. He listened again. Isabelle-Marie's sobs were not those of a woman; they were like the moans of a stricken animal. But Patrice did not care. The air rushed into his chest; the cool earth swelled beneath his feet. He started running, moist at the temples. When he arrived at the edge of the lake, like a child looking for a sequel to an endless game of make-believe, he grew quiet again, watching his face, his arms, and his neck, miraculously reflected in the water. Comforted, he fell asleep.

Isabelle-Marie was cutting the bread with a feverish hand. She did not tear it apart as a child would but cut straight through with cold dispatch. Louise saw anger gleam in the corners of her eyes and her mouth and press her cheeks into hollows of discontent.

'Why are you hiding the bread in your apron, Isabelle?'

Isabelle-Marie pinched her lips and held out the bread, all the while staring at Louise.

'Here, Mother,' she said, then added scornfully, 'I made this bread myself so I know that it's good.'

Louise had learned to endure the sting of her glances, their piercing hatred; only in the eyes of her daughter could a glance be so cutting. She resigned herself to this bit by bit, as though to a private, unmentionable agony.

'Another piece for Patrice,' she said.

Meals were a time of naked exposure. Hands reached out, revealing trembling fingers. Faces met in grave collisions. Isabelle-Marie saw her mother and her mother's son radiant with health, and felt herself becoming uglier as Patrice grew in adolescent beauty.

'My children,' said Louise, though she looked only at Patrice when she spoke, 'I have decided to take a trip. I would like to discuss the latest farm equipment with some friends. You see, with fewer workers and more . . .'

Isabelle-Marie listened, frigid and unresponsive.

Louise spoke more quickly, 'Will you come with me, Patrice?'

When he did not answer, she said, 'Oh, I understand, it wouldn't be much fun for a boy of your age . . .'

She was trying brazenly and yet skilfully to guide the responses of this Beautiful Beast, this bewitching creature whom people pointed out in the streets. The dazzling beauty of her child filled everyone with wonder, and she savored this, voluptuously.

Patrice muttered 'No' in a kind of wistful pout that only Louise understood. Then he dug his teeth into a piece of bread. The way he ate had a charming, slightly untamed quality. His eyes sparkled, his cheekbones glowed with vitality.

'The idea doesn't appeal to you, does it, my dearest? Well then, I will go alone. You can rest at home.'

Rest. He did nothing else. He lived by resting, at the expense of other people. He sucked their blood . . . in order to rest.

'Isabelle-Marie will take care of you. She is a real woman now, you know. She can bake excellent bread when she wants to.'

'Yes,' said Isabelle-Marie. Her reply was much too abrupt, too final.

She bit her lip. Something was shrieking inside of her . . . an evil desire.

'Isabelle-Marie, what is the matter, Isabelle-Marie?'

The anguish which she had felt that day on the train was coming over her again. She held her hand against her mouth and grew purple with rage.

'That is an excellent idea, Mother. We need some good ploughs. The soil is hard to work these days.'

Louise saw that she was trembling, though she did not understand why.

Louise set off by herself. She would miss her child. Without him she was lost, shorn of both roots and flowers. At forty, Louise was still a frivolous doll, empty and excessively concerned with her slender body. Patrice's beauty was to her but a reflection of her own.

She also needed the false security of luxury. Luxury! She craved it. Her pleasures were those of someone who had grown neither wiser nor stronger through suffering. Though she was not intelligent and had the soul of a mannequin, in her veins ran a streak of foresight and cunning. Her daughter exasperated her. 'Can you expect anything but trouble from someone so ugly?' And yet Isabelle-Marie took after her father, that gallant dreamer and poet who used to speak of his land as though of a virgin consecrated to God. How could such a man have felt passionate about Louise, with her flighty, skin-deep beauty? Because Louise knew how to pounce on vulnerable spirits, taken by her charms. She used her body with the single-minded determination of a prostitute, and had the same obsession with money.

Isabelle-Marie was ten years old when her father died. Since then she had withdrawn into her sorrow, and contempt for Louise had shriveled her soul.

Louise set off by herself. Separated for the first time in her life from Patrice, she felt severed in two.

'I want some bread, give me some bread, Isabelle.'

At noon the table was bright with sunshine but the faces were pale. Isabelle-Marie hid the bread in her apron, standing in front of Patrice who, in his desperation, looked more and more like himself, like an idiot. At last Isabelle-Marie was free not to fear her brother. She could try anything; he knew no way of defending himself.

By depriving him of food she could make him pale and wan, and this creature who had never known the touch of misery would become her puppet, her own spindly puppet. Yes, Isabelle-Marie wanted to make him ugly. For a moment she shied away from this perverse desire, then she gave in to it. Oh, to watch the slow disintegration of his beauty! Was this a crime? But why? . . . Did Patrice deserve his beauty?

The poison burst within her and she was amazed by her own strength. And what about me? . . . Is it my fault that I am ugly?

Patrice held out both hands and looked around as though seeking his mother, needing her shoulder.

'I'm hungry, I'm hungry.'

He went on tormenting his sister, pleading with her in a trembling voice while she, carried away by her new power, shoved him with her elbow and disappeared with the bread, as though she were protecting a child from fire or undeserved punishment.

Patrice did not know how to fight back. He hugged himself and cried.

Mercilessly, Isabelle-Marie resisted his laments. Then, like a feeble, daydreaming child, Patrice fell into a gentle sleep, his stomach empty and hollow, such a gentle sleep that it was barely sleep at all.

The first few nights he woke screaming, hammering his fists against the door until a strange kind of death finally came over him. He collapsed, and 'rested.' At other times, in delirium, he would go out and run around the garden like a madman. He held out his arms and raced toward the lake, where he plunged his feverish face and his whole famished body into the water.

His suffering was great, but he reacted to it like an idiot.

He devoured whatever he could find in the fields, rolling in the grass, abandoning himself to his terrible hunger. On the fourth day, Isabelle-Marie found him less dazzling. There were rings under his eyes and his lips were purplish. Having half succeeded in her revenge, she lost interest. On the fifth day she saw her brother lying near the door, his chest swollen outward, very still. He wore a vague smile. She looked at him for a long time, until her soul could stand it no longer.

'After all, Patrice is only a child.'

She lifted him, but his weight was more than she could bear. She laid him over her knees, mournfully, as though he were dying.

Isabelle-Marie began to rock her brother back and forth. His white body lay in her arms with one limp hand around her neck. He rested his face against her with his eyes closed, instinctively accepting any shoulder as a refuge for his innocent brow. Abandoning himself thus to Isabelle-Marie, he was seeking the warmth of his mother. Isabelle-Marie did not try to raise him to his feet.

The three mountains were reflected in the lake like phantom swimmers. The strange chill which permeates the shore rose beneath Isabelle-Marie's feet and she stared into the distance, without moving, in no way afraid of this living statue that slept on, as if attached to her thigh. Patrice was breathing with difficulty. His was the sickly sleep of an invalid who has reached the end of a desperate crisis. His lower lip curved into a smile, but it was only the half-smile of suffering, all the more distressing on a face that was never troubled. Isabelle-Marie noticed the dust in his luxurious hair and the blotches on his bloodless cheeks. But his forehead kept its youthful pride, an admirable, guiltless forehead which she now held against her shoulder with more compassion. Patrice would probably always be handsome and empty. But some of his strength was gone. Isabelle-Marie ran her hand through her brother's hair and laughed as she shook him.

'Are you asleep, my child?'

She watched for the faint quivers of fear in his thick lashes.

'You know, my child, I feel sorry for you.'

But he was not listening. It would be so easy to claw this innocent face that did not struggle, to unleash her fiendish nails upon him, but she withdrew her hand and bit her lip. Then she laughed as she ruffled his hair in a wild burst of tenderness.

'My Beautiful Beast . . . oh, my Beautiful Beast!'

Patrice shuddered. He was hungry. His body was very warm as it rested against his sister's flesh. She pretended to be casual.

'Why then, get up! I'll give you some bread, my Beautiful Beast, of course I will. Stand up!'

But he could not stand alone. Isabelle took him in her arms and carried him with his head over her shoulder, like a child who has fainted. She thought how simple it would be to walk out into the lake and lower her brother into the water, to drown this near-corpse.

Then coming to her senses, she thought, After all, even an animal has a right to live.

Wandering in the woods, she wept, suddenly sorry for what she had done, or was it rather the poignancy she felt in carrying in her arms a body without a soul? Louise's great hero no longer weighed as much as a man. He was ephemeral and pure, already beyond suffering. Clasping his body to her, Isabelle-Marie ran back to the house, consumed by a passionate instinct to protect her brother.

When she arrived, she was dripping with perspiration, and her ankle was slightly bruised.

And now she did not know how to make Patrice well again. Nor did he try to help himself. Louise had coddled her son so much that he was quite unprepared for Isabelle-Marie's cruelty. So Patrice lingered in fever and delirium, without any desire to eat. He lay dreaming, white between white sheets. In his imagination, all the water left the lake. He found himself looking for his reflection in the disappearing water and cried out, but no mirror reflected his face nor echoed his cry. At night, when he heard his sister's sobbing, he thrashed in his bed.

Frantic at the approaching return of her mother, Isabelle-Marie was even more stricken, more heartbroken. The faintest murmur of distress brought her to Patrice's bedside, where she sponged his brow, soothed him, and offered him cool drinks. The boy distrusted his sister deeply, with the blind fear of a slave. Only his own reflection made him feel secure. In the midst of his worst nightmares, Isabelle-Marie would bring him a mirror, and he would smile at his perfect teeth, his pure mouth. An illusion of peace held him spellbound, though it did not cure him.

Patrice wasted away languidly, as though savoring his own misfortune.

'Drink, Patrice, please drink.'

His lips seemed defiant in their laziness. He smoothed the sheets and sank gently against the pillows. A miracle was transfiguring his features, one by one, into a new and disturbing kind of beauty. Isabelle-Marie thought that her victim had been rescued from evil and ugliness, because privation had subjected Patrice to the strange magic of death, in which all faces are beautiful.

Though thin, he was dazzling. Though young, she was withered.

'Mother will come back,' begged Patrice. 'Won't she?'

'Of course she will, my Beautiful Beast, and you will be happy again.'

Suddenly she began to scrutinize him with her dark eyes, as though she were holding him between her gaze and her mouth, as though she did not want this creature, who even yet did not know suffering, to escape from her clutches.

'Would you like a little wine?'

He did not answer. Hallucinations made him tremble again, and he began to perspire, to cry out, his mouth pressed against Isabelle-Marie's shoulder.

'Come now, be a good boy.'

He drowned the girl's bare neck in burning tears, clutched at her waist, and Isabelle-Marie experienced an excruciating longing to die, to disappear in the shadows.

She then found that part of her desire to hurt her brother was a masochistic fear that she would lose him. But the boy still lingered on in delicious lethargy.

Isabelle-Marie devoted herself to him night and day, at once fearing and enjoying his famished cries. Patrice grew thinner.

One day when the pain was more excruciating than ever, when Isabelle-Marie began to fear a final night of agony, Louise arrived, tall, rested, a flaming red hat on her dyed hair. The trip had given her skin the inviting glow of a woman who is just mature enough to be beautiful.

But she was not alone; with her was an elegantly dressed man of her own age. Standing before them, Isabelle-Marie wore a faint smile. For a number of years now, her mother had been promising the arrival of this friend, whom she described as being of 'well-sculptured and manly build.'

'Oh, Isabelle-Marie, how sad you look!'

Then her voice suddenly changed.

'Where is Patrice? Have you met my son, Lanz? There has never been a child like him. My friends say that only a genius could be so beautiful!'

'Patrice . . . Patrice,' she called, cupping her gloved hands.

Isabelle-Marie stood firmly in front of her.

'He is asleep, Mother.'

Louise rested her head on the shoulder of her exquisite admirer. He seemed unconcerned.

'Asleep. He must have been running too much again. I knew it! By the way, Lanz, you haven't met my daughter Isabelle.'

Isabelle-Marie did not hold out her hand. The look in Lanz's eyes reminded her of how ugly she was.

'Lanz,' Louise continued in a melting voice. 'You must excuse my daughter. She is a savage; no discipline ever had any effect on her.'

She laughed, showing off her deceitful mouth. Isabelle-Marie noticed nervous lines beneath her make-up, and a tiny vein which ran from her eye to her delicate nose, like a tear of blood.

'We must wake him,' said Louise.

'He is very sick.'

Louise faltered, but found renewed strength in the presence of her admirer. She began to pull the gloves from her fingers, with elegant, deliberately slow gestures.

She turned back again, her face suddenly soured and wrinkled by this unexpected sorrow.

'Patrice is sick?'

As she crossed the room, she took off her hat and let her hands fall to her sides. She stopped on the threshold.

'Patrice, Patrice, what is the matter?'

Lying on his back like a marble god, pale, with his mouth half open, Patrice stared at his mother. Louise suddenly felt lacerated and oppressed.

She threw herself upon him. She could feel his feverish body beneath her own.

'Patrice, my dearest, what is the matter? I'll never go away again, not ever. I'll always come back to you. But I am back now. Patrice . . . Patrice . . .'

Patrice cried plaintively into her hair. Louise caressed him as though he were a corpse.

'What happened, Patrice? Please tell me.'

'I can't remember.'

Isabelle-Marie listened. Her brother would not tell. His impoverished mind would protect her. She laughed inside herself and, for a moment, a gleam of perversity shone in her eyes. Lanz was disturbed to see such coarse features and this body as mean as a dented sword. He twirled the little gold cane which he used, with infinite grace, to support his lame leg. This infirmity, which enhanced his proud bearing and broad shoulders, captured the essence of his vanity. Isabelle-Marie found him more virile and impressive in profile. A ray of sunshine gave his dark beard the look of an unfinished mask. Behind this he hid the cruelty of his eyes, the falsely masculine expression of a man who knows no other role to play in life but that of a man of fashion.

Isabelle-Marie was repelled at the thought that this creature was her mother's lover, for she considered Louise too absurd to inspire any kind of desire, even a physical one. Lanz disgusted her. She passed judgment upon him. Hadn't she the privilege of passing judgment upon those who contributed to her suffering?

A cold sweat bathed her brow; she wiped it away with a frantic gesture and leaned her head against the casement of the door. She heard Patrice's squeals, little cries of delight like those of a young animal. She almost fainted, the way she had years before, when Patrice was being admired on the train. Her body became rigid. Then she grew calm again.

Louise was appalled. She bent over her son, begging him not to die. He fell asleep, warmed by her breath, having finally found in his mother the mirror he had been seeking.

'Isabelle,' shrieked Louise, 'I know what was wrong with this child! Me! He needed me . . .'

Isabelle-Marie sneered and disappeared across the fields.

While Louise resurrected her Beautiful Beast, Patrice became suspicious of Lanz. He did not know why he disliked this intruder, but he instinctively felt threatened.

When she was not listening to Lanz talking about his clothes, Louise took her dazzling son on walks, showing him off, boasting about him. Between Lanz, who was excited by her skilfully made-up appearance, and Patrice, who was pleased by everything she did without ever understanding it, Louise's every desire was satisfied.

When they came to the edge of the garden, Patrice and his mother entered a long avenue of willows. Louise saw Isabelle-Marie emerge from this immense green chalice with her three dogs and then disappear again, her hair flying in the wind. She wondered why her daughter always wore black

dresses . . . They cling to her hips like a shroud, she thought.
Then she looked at Patrice and was comforted. She taught
him to swing his body gracefully as he walked, content so
long as she possessed this youthful beauty, even though it
was beauty devoid of intelligence.

Since her return, she had been teaching Patrice to take an
interest in his own person, to make himself attractive, physically perfect. She could make him into whatever she wanted,
and this made her feel more like a mother.

'Why is it, Mother, that Isabelle is always running about
like this?'

'How should I know? Your sister loves to work. Don't
you remember, even when she was very small she loved to
help with the harvesting.'

As she said this, she laughed, and her laugh evoked the
doom of invalids and consumptives. Some of her grace went
beyond elegance and hinted at illness.

'What fine cheeks you have, Patrice! And your hands are
no longer idle; they are a man's hands . . . And such a strong
neck . . . The sun will tan it and make it healthy.'

She talked on and on and Patrice did not notice the little
streak on his mother's face, the sinister tendril that clawed
its way along the flesh, marring the white skin a bit more
every day. In spite of this Louise felt secure, but this security
was slowly undermining her strength. She basked in the admiration of others like a pretty doll, never for a moment
suspecting that one day she would lie battered and abandoned.

Suddenly she found herself alone. Patrice was running . . .
It was as though he were inventing his own private ballet,
a dancing beam of sunshine from a sun within himself.

Louise cried out, 'Now don't get excited, Patrice . . . Come
back here!'

Patrice ran about beneath the trees, ecstatically bending
and stretching, caressing the burgeoning ground with his
bare hands.

33

Now he stood still again, next to Isabelle-Marie, with his head against the wall, his eyes lifted, deep in silence. He was looking at his mother; bathed in light, she seemed to float toward the forest. Lanz raised her from the ground simply by holding her hand; a glass hand, thought Isabelle-Marie. Lanz was laughing gaily as he walked along, pushing the grass aside with his little gold cane. Sometimes he twirled this baton so skilfully that his lameness seemed no more than a dapper affectation. As he threw his head backward, his beard framed the pallor of his delicate features and his smooth skin which seemed made for a woman to hold between her hands.

He was easy-going and always accommodating. Neither good nor evil, fierce nor gentle, he did not really know what he was; nor did he try to find out. Like Louise he was swayed by vain, artificial desires. He liked wine, gluttony, and stupid, easy women. He adored the giddy feeling of being surrounded by conquests: the irresistible seducer. Totally without scruples, he made love to many women, charming one and then another, fashioning sublime but meaningless compliments for each one, and finally leaving behind him a wake of bleeding hearts about which he would boast outrageously.

'At least,' he said, 'someone will have cried for me.'

Louise was like an old doll. She belonged to him. Louise had found an adorer, and Lanz had found adoration, each as futile and ill-fated as the other.

Isabelle-Marie blew on the nape of her brother's neck. He trembled slightly and his breast, which was as chaste as his brow, quivered like the breast of a child.

"Look at them. Lanz is her son now; Lanz is the one who walks with her; Lanz takes care of the horses. You aren't her dear Patrice any more.'

'Say that again, slowly,' said Patrice who did not understand.

'I said that Mother does not love you any more, Patrice.'

'Me?'

'Yes, you.'

Patrice, who already harbored a wordless animosity toward Lanz, suddenly felt a wild desire to scream, and he screamed, with tears dripping from his eyelashes.

'Patrice . . . Don't you feel well, Patrice?' asked Isabelle-Marie in a deceitful tone of voice.

He gazed in misery at the unfaithful ones, as they strolled between the trees, arms twined about one another. His eyeballs were swollen with sadness and protruded in horror like those of a madman.

'Let's go home now,' said Isabelle-Marie. 'I was only teasing. Just a little joke between us. Will you help me wash the dishes?'

He did not answer. His skin did not show even a tremor.

'Come with me, please,' she begged, surprised that he was so gullible.

Patrice fled. He was sixteen and he could run better than a skilled athlete. Before he disappeared, Isabelle-Marie had time to be hurt again by his beauty.

'Where are you going?'

She, too, started running, but as she tried to catch up with her brother, everything inside of her began to tear apart.

When he reached the lake Patrice waited for the water to bring him peace. He looked at his reflection and then rose, very slowly, holding out his arms as though trying to drink of his own beauty, drop by drop until there was no more. He was alone and magnificent, as he stood ready to leap into the setting sun.

5

One night Patrice walked into his mother's room to say good night, at the hour when Louise usually wandered dreamily between the mirror and the window, pulling the combs from her hair. But this time Louise was not there. The gold cane had been left across the open covers of the bed and a man's glove lay in the middle of the sheets. Lanz's silk handkerchiefs hung everywhere, each with a different scent. Though he did not know why, Patrice took fright. Suddenly the room no longer offered the velvet warmth, the arms that opened and closed and embraced. He looked around in despair, no longer finding any security. The gold cane reminded him of Lanz and of his walk that afternoon, and also Lanz's beard, and Lanz's eyes which he feared. Patrice hardly even dared sit on the edge of the bed. He felt as though he were being crushed by the walls. Everything was different. He stood there without moving, uneasy and bewildered, engulfed by a hostile presence.

He felt a bitter need to beg for mercy, but his own feelings were as confusing to him as his soul.

Next door, on a farm which belonged to a large, happy family, a party was being given, and Patrice could hear the singing. It filled him with melancholy. For a moment he forgot the gold cane and the silk handkerchiefs and even the glove that belonged to old Lanz. He leaned close to the damp shutters, letting his sadness merge with the evening shadows. Over there, girls and boys were dancing, kissing, and shouting songs of youth. Patrice listened and marveled, his mind drowned deeper than ever in troubled waters.

He had never known any human beings except his mother, his fly-by-night tutors, and Isabelle-Marie. Other people only admired him as they passed. They never looked back to find out what they had seen. Then, too, Louise protected him from everyone else in order to strengthen her own hold upon him. This was not hard for her to do.

Alone in his room, Patrice danced and imitated, for he always imitated everything, the gestures of the young couples. He danced and laughed as he danced, feeling an urge for speed throb within him. Isabelle-Marie would have loved to dance like this, but Isabelle-Marie was ashamed and worked in the fields where no one could see her, talking to the animals who would never insult and wound her, the way people did. Confused, Patrice closed the shutters against this night that sang like cicadas, and his gaze again took in the unmade bed, the white sheets, the glove . . . and Lanz's hateful cane. He felt a strange contempt, half-masculine, half-childish, and his dilated nostrils made his mask of pride into a mask of rebellion.

He looked for Louise's hair which to him was a soft cloth on which he could dry his tears of woe. He saw a tall man in the mirror: himself. He touched the glass with the tip of his fingernail and smiled, but was not satisfied. He went back to the bed. Louise would say, 'Come here, let me take those leaves out of your hair,' or 'How you have grown, Patrice!' but this evening she was silent. Everything was silent. Patrice knelt on the floor with his head buried in the sheets and sobbed like a starving child. He cried and cried, and the sight of this fair adolescent with his shoulders trembling, convulsed by despair, was pitiful.

Louise and Lanz came into the room.

Louise blanched beneath her make-up and the mark on her cheek seemed redder.

'Help me, Lanz. Patrice is feverish. He's sick again. I can tell.'

Lanz obeyed and sponged Patrice's brow but the poor idiot clung all the harder to Louise, weeping on his mother's neck.

'What is the matter? Tell me . . .' murmured Louise.

He did not answer. Suddenly he rose to his feet and started to run away but Lanz kept him back with one bare hand, holding his other gloved hand behind his back.

'Are you in pain, Patrice?'

Patrice looked back with an expression that disturbed Lanz . . . Lanz, who never paid attention to anything but himself and his world of dolls. Isabelle-Marie had often asked herself how a creature as egotistical as Lanz could be capable of any normal emotions. But now he felt naked under Patrice's stare. 'What could such an expression mean?' he wondered. 'Has he any intelligence, or is he unhappy because he has none?'

Then, smoothing his eyebrows, he announced in a worldly tone of voice, 'Patrice, we have something to tell you. Louise and I are going to be married. Does this make you smile? Look, Louise, he is smiling. He isn't sick at all.'

He was right. Patrice was smiling, for he did not understand. Louise clasped him to her bosom and praised him. She laughed, and her cheeks glowed.

'Bring the glasses and we'll all drink together!'

'Isabelle-Marie, where are you, Isabelle-Marie?'

Patrice was left alone in the room. A tear fell on his pouting lips.

'Isabelle-Marie, you must celebrate with us. I am almost your father now.'

'Drink to us, Isabelle-Marie!' said Louise; then, more tenderly, 'Patrice, why are you biting your nails?'

Patrice lifted his glass and struck it mechanically against Lanz's in a gesture that meant nothing to him.

'Why are you always so quiet, Patrice?'

'He has nothing to say,' snapped Isabelle-Marie. She, too, looked glum.

No one heard her. She was not quite so frightening this evening. She had tied a white scarf over her black dress and had used a little lipstick. She too was listening to the wild music which came from the farm next door.

'Isabelle-Marie, what are you thinking about?'

'Isabelle-Marie, bring some more wine.'

Her body stiffened.

She thought of the approaching marriage of this pair of dolls, a male doll and a female doll. She would have to live in the midst of this depravity—the artificial depravity of faces in the movies. How sad, she thought, they have no souls.

Far off in her childhood, she could see her father, the austere peasant, the maker of bread. When he tilled the virgin loins of the earth, he was penetrating to the heart of God. In his soul, honesty mingled with instinct, just as good wine mellowed his complexion.

Isabelle-Marie remembered her father's enormous boots, which smelled of wheat and loam.

'Why, Isabelle-Marie, you are all pink! Something has finally turned you into a young girl . . . Is it the wine?'

Isabelle-Marie did not hear her mother. Louise was confusing her various roles; first she abandoned Patrice for her lover and then Lanz for Patrice. She laughed, enjoying these two beautiful heads, and sometimes Patrice nuzzled his forehead against her shoulder while Lanz amused himself elsewhere. He amused himself everywhere . . . he, Lanz! . . . so strangely fresh and youthful. He laughed, and his laughter was the graceful, congealed laughter of marionettes. That was all there was to Lanz. He was elegant; even his laughter was elegant.

And so the dolls met and were united, without needing to know one another. Patrice stood by, sparkling with innocence.

Overcome, quivering with the same anguish as that day on the train, Isabelle-Marie left the room.

6

In the middle of the night she suddenly turned over in bed and felt consumed with pleasure, imagining that she was beautiful. Next door she heard shouting. Circles of young people were dancing under the lighted trees, the girls spinning round and round, ethereal in their beribboned dresses. Isabelle-Marie ran to join them.

The dancing was so fast that her cheek struck other faces and she was thrown from arm to arm, exhilarated, awkward, emancipated by the torrents within her. She danced wildly, endangering her weak ankle, which had been thinner than the other since she was born.

She immersed herself in this crowd of young people, withdrawing and then reappearing, like a woman released from purdah for one night. Her thighs burned. She danced in a frenzy, scrawny and twisted, depleted by the very joy she savored.

As a child she had often frequented cemeteries, wandering from cross to cross, cultivating her melancholy in the doleful breezes. Since then, bitter and diabolical reveries had haunted her every thought, until now her anguished soul was reflected, rather frighteningly, on her face.

But that night she danced so much that she no longer knew who she was. Suddenly a young arm stopped her. She waltzed on one foot, the way one would dance over daggers, looking at the ground.

'You there, you are dancing too much.'

Isabelle-Marie fastened her severe gaze on the person who had said this to her. It was a young man of eighteen. He was laughing hilariously. When he stopped, he lifted his beautiful head and she saw his curly, pure-white hair. His eyes were black, a very soft black, set in a hollow beneath his brow, with a look of permanent disdain in their pupils like the disdain in the eyes of a misbegotten child. Isabelle-Marie flinched under his stare. Then she showed her surprise, none too gently.

'Is your hair really white? Am I dreaming?'

He laughed even harder.

'No, you are not dreaming. My hair is so blond that it is white.'

Then, silently caressing her face, the boy ran his outspread fingers over the cheeks and the mute throat of the girl before him. He laid his hand on Isabelle-Marie's shoulder, where the gangling bones were joined together.

'You are very beautiful,' he said finally.

She pushed him away, wanting to escape and dance again with the others, but his weird expression held her back. When he told her that she was beautiful, she had given him a quick hug. He laughed again, like someone born to laugh, and to die at dawn.

Then, breathing heavily against her eager cheek, he said, 'You must excuse me; I am blind.'

Then she understood everything, his aloof bearing, his eyes that seemed to wander in darkness. Only a blind man could 'see' her as beautiful. So she decided to play at being beautiful. She vowed this to herself as the girls with the ribbons threw flowers at the boys.

Her face grew pale again as she drew herself together and said, 'Yes, I am very beautiful. I have violet eyes and long blond hair. Feel my hair. It has the aroma of newly baked bread, hasn't it?'

He smiled, dazzling and deceived.

'Are you really so beautiful?'

'I am a little bit too thin.'

Then, clutching her arm and burying his forehead in her black hair, he said, 'Soon I will be able to look at you. I will be able to see you. My eyes are being treated. They promised me, and I believe them. Once I could see nothing but blackness, then lines; now I can see shadows. The light will come, I know.'

'But why does it matter? You don't have to see me, since you know I am beautiful.'

'I assure you . . . some day I will see.'

'I will still be beautiful.'

She spoke nervously, already worried about her lies.

'Would you like to dance?'

They danced. Isabelle-Marie breathed again; she felt at peace. A fragile soul came alive within her. She clasped him more tightly. I have brought him hope, she said to herself. Because of me he has hope!

'Why are you hurting me so? Let's walk now. Let's not dance any more. I must go home. I have a sick friend. I mean . . . my brother. I must take care of him.'

He followed her as far as the farmhouse. He skipped as he walked, here and there breaking off a twig and snapping it between his teeth. Isabelle-Marie would have given anything to keep this hand in hers for a long time.

He asked in a quiet voice, 'What is your name?'

'Isabelle-Marie.'

'Isabelle, Is-a-belle. Isa the Beautiful,' he murmured.

Then he kissed her furtively, barely on the mouth.

'Mine is Michael.'

They stumbled over a tree trunk and let themselves fall, lying next to one another on the ground. The damp grass penetrated their clothes. They did not move. Isabelle-Marie spoke of the green moon as though it were a jewel from the same hoard as her violet eyes. She wanted to be in love, to be beautiful. Both of them were pure, for in them burned a longing for perfect beauty. They did not speak. Dogs bayed in the distance and the echoes of the dance could be heard above their baying.

'Will you always be mine, Isabelle-Marie?'

'Always.'

She said 'Yes' without trembling, holding her breath. She bit her lip. 'Yes, I will always be beautiful.'

'Why are you leaving?'

'I must go home. My brother is waiting for me.'

7

When she arrived home, Isabelle-Marie discovered her
brother standing alone in a heap of broken glass, with blood
on his clothes.

'What have you done?'

He pouted and wrinkled his forehead, and his eyebrows
came together like satin fingers.

'I broke the glasses.'

'Where is Mother? And Lanz?'

He waved his arm in the direction of the forest. He was
weary and his nonchalance revealed why.

'They are walking in the forest,' he said.

'You drank too much.'

'I broke the goblets because I wanted to break them.'

Patrice lived entirely through his senses. When there was
no one to hug him, he had to console himself with noise.

'Look at your finger. Come here, let me fix it for you.'

He hid his bloody hand in his shirt, taking a stance like a
boxer who fends off blows with one shoulder.

'There is nothing wrong with me.'

'Come here, Beautiful Beast. Are you afraid of me?'

He lowered his head.

'Yes.'

He saw the blood on his skin. One drop was enough to ter-
rify him.

'Take it away, quickly, take it away!'

Isabelle-Marie swathed his wounded hand in a napkin.

'There is no light in here. But outside . . . outside . . .'

'I would like to dance with all the girls.'

Isabelle-Marie laughed feebly. Patrice closed his eyes and
rested his head on her shoulder.

'It is nothing, Patrice. Just a little cut. But we don't break glasses like that. If Mother knew! Only babies do such things, Patrice!'

Patrice leaned even harder against his sister.

'Mother doesn't pay attention to me any more. Do you think the man with the gold cane will be here for a long time?'

'For a lifetime.'

'A lifetime?'

'I mean "forever." As long as there is water in the lake.'

'Is that true?'

'Yes, it is true.'

'It's not a joke?'

'I never joke.'

'Then that is much too long,' said Patrice, straightening himself slightly, wild-eyed with despair. He felt like running and never stopping. Isabelle-Marie sensed this.

'Don't go. I will give you a bath, the way Mother does after you have been sick, and then you can climb into a nice warm bed. Patrice? Are you crying?'

He was sitting on the floor again, playing with bits of glass.

'I would like to run and run and break glasses and cut myself all over and then Mother would come back from the forest.'

'Stupid,' said Isabelle-Marie. 'He is her husband now, don't you know what a husband is?'

'No,' he answered, shaking his head.

'A husband is a man a woman stays with forever. Do you understand? She is like his mother. Louise is now Lanz's mother.'

He arched his back in self-defence.

'No. She is my mother, only mine.'

She slapped his wrist and the pieces of glass fell, one by one.

'I said stop it. Do you want to see your fingers bleed again?'

45

'She is my mother.'

She shrugged her shoulders, unable to explain.

'My Beautiful Beast! My poor Beautiful Beast!'

The way she was laughing surprised Patrice.

'Are you happy?'

'Yes, I danced all night.'

Now that hope had begun to fill Isabelle-Marie's heart, Patrice's beauty no longer made her suffer. She rose and danced around the room.

'And I will dance again, Patrice! When the Livanis' second daughter turns twenty. At their parties all the young people sing and dance and drink champagne.'

Patrice was kneeling among the splinters of broken glass; he was not listening.

'What do Lanz and Mother talk about in the woods?

'Not about you. They dream that they are twenty again.'

Patrice wanted to lie down and cry, with his arms folded under his forehead . . . or to run.

'Patrice, don't go. I thought you weren't afraid of me any more.'

'I'm all right. I just feel hot. And Mother, I want to find Mother.'

She had drawn a bath and laid out clean clothes. She knew that Patrice liked fresh, perfumed linen. She helped him to his feet.

'It isn't good for you to drink like this. Didn't Mother tell you so?'

'No. She gave me lots to drink. And Lanz gave me more.'

So Lanz had made Patrice drunk, to distract him from his mother. He was disgusting.

"Come, my Beautiful Beast. You see, you can't even walk alone. What would you do without me?'

'The bread . . .'

'What bread?'

'The bread you hid from me. I was so hungry . . .'

46

'You are imagining things, Patrice. I never hid any bread from you.'

'Then it is just something in the back of my head.'

'Yes, in the back of your head.'

She undressed him, holding him in her arms. When he raised his eyes to look at her, his expression was so pathetic that she could have cried.

Can a Beautiful Beast have feelings? she wondered.

Above his lithe body, Patrice's face was contorted. He seemed to have forgotten how to move his limbs.

8

Louise, inwardly torn, gave less of herself to Patrice than to her husband, and whenever she revealed her desire to give more to Patrice Lanz interfered with cunning displays of false tenderness.

The faded lovers lived happily. They walked and hunted, and in the evening they played chess, more relaxed in the lamplight.

Patrice dreaded his mother's room and the gold cane repelled him. Sometimes he would harness the horses and take refuge in the forest and, in his innocent despair, he often threw himself fully clothed into the lake.

Isabelle-Marie lost her passion for work in the fields. She became more feminine, less agonized. At dawn, before feeding the animals, with the dew on her bare shoulders, she would go to meet Michael by the Livanis' farm. She was entirely transformed and wore white dresses with flowers at the waist.

'I am more beautiful today than yesterday.'

Then Michael would ask, burying his face in the fragrance of her neck, 'Are your eyes violet?'

'Yes.'

'And is your body very white?'

'Yes.'

But her eyes were black and mean, and her skin was like a tanned hide. She stroked his hair. Michael thrilled to her caresses.

'Soon I will see you. I can already make out the outlines of your body, just the outlines. You are very tall, I know that.'

She thought to herself, He is a dreamer. He will certainly never be able to see.'

'When I was ten years old, one of my cats struck me with her claws.'

She was not listening. His long eyelashes were of the same pure whiteness as his hair, as if touched by the same snow, and under these lashes his gaze seemed blade-sharp, candid, not quite human.

Isabelle-Marie had been fascinated from the beginning by his mauve mouth. It was like two halves of a piece of fruit. She was glad that he was blind, like her a creature of the earth but with eyes cut off from the light and with sable markings on his chest. Since she was quick to take hold of any situation, she immediately accepted Michael's infirmity. Hand in hand, they walked to the other side of the lake, where the three mountains began. There they ran, pure and innocent.

Wishing to be beautiful will probably make me beautiful, thought Isabelle-Marie, to justify her 'game.'

They ran barefoot, impatient and unbridled. They had the whole forest and nature itself in which to play games of youth and love. They were eighteen. A wealth of physical well-being was theirs to squander, as everything is squandered at their age, even passion and genius. They were innocent; they were virgins. They enjoyed an intimate cameraderie which sanctioned everything but spared them the wounds of the flesh, unlike others who live before they have discovered the magic of life.

Unaware of this miracle, Lanz and Louise continued their jaded dialogue. Isabelle-Marie turned her back on the jealousy which had tortured her heart for so long and learned the joy of being a woman. A woman who is happy to have arms, a mouth, a face that reflects everything, above all a woman who has a heart. Michael was like a young animal. He was hungry for joy, intolerant of ugliness, and repelled by suffering. He was proud, poetic, and full of illusions, for he lived only in dreams. He knew the woods, the lake, and the cycles of the harvest, but he could not write his name.

49

The faintest rustling told him what kind of animal had stirred.

'That was a rabbit, wasn't it?'

'Yes, a rabbit,' said Isabelle-Marie, beaming.

He intensified everything with his enthusiasm.

'Listen . . . a storm is coming.'

'Do you think so?'

Later, the rain fell on them, as they sank, crazy with laughter, among the flowers. But they were not idle very often. Their energy, the fire in their veins, drove them to race through the woods until they were exhausted. They strayed, parted for a few hours, and then the first one to gather an armful of flowers called out, sending echoes between the lake and the trees. When Isabelle-Marie went home, she was so happy, so alive that her mother did not recognize her.

'One would think Isabelle-Marie has taken to drink,' she said to her husband who was leaning on his gold cane, swathed in voluminous silk scarves.

Sometimes Louise would dare to ask, 'Where is Patrice?' and Lanz would answer curtly, 'I saw him on horseback this afternoon.'

Carried away by her new adventures, Isabelle-Marie had forgotten her brother. And so Patrice, who had always had the hatred of his sister and the overpowering love of his mother, lost both at the same time. He was abandoned, and he sensed it.

'Is he with the horses again?'

'He is ruining them,' Lanz declared. 'When he rides, he hangs on to the horse's neck as though he were afraid of losing it.'

The beautiful Patrice now had only his horses, his wild, morbid racing, and his image in the water. Louise still flattered him in Lanz's presence, but more moderately. Lanz was slowly smothering her maternal instincts in order to take complete possession of his wife, even though it might make her suffer. They spent whole days and nights together, in a savage exchange of bodies, as though offering flesh to be eaten. They were vile, unwholesome. Isabelle-Marie thought them depraved, unworthy. For in her heart of hearts, Isabelle-Marie was like her brother: a creature of innate purity.

'It is past midnight, Lanz . . . Patrice is not home yet.'

Lanz's cane was hooked in the hollow of his elbow. He sat smoking in the lamplight, his face blotched with grey, eroded by elegance. He opened his mouth to puff the smoke and his white teeth appeared, glistening with saliva.

'Watch out, Louise, check.' He leaned back in his chair so that the light fell on his beard.

'That was foolish! What are you doing? You will never learn.'

Louise, pouting childishly under her make-up, was holding her hand poised above the chessboard. She was neither skilful nor interested. When the lamplight fell on the side of her face, it revealed the vein Isabelle-Marie had noticed, puckering her whole cheek.

Louise covered this cheek with the back of her hand.

'Louise, a little effort . . . please.'

'But why? You always win.'

Her delicately outlined eyelid trembled; she stared at the clock.

'After midnight and Patrice . . .'

Lanz burst out in anger, 'Patrice, Patrice, always Patrice!'

Then, lowering his voice, 'But Louise, whatever are you doing? Have you forgotten how to play?'

She wrinkled her nose and tried to find a way to look attractive as she pondered the game. But all she could manage was a distorted grin.

'No, no, not that way,' he pleaded, smoke curling from the corner of his mouth.

'I am going out to the woods, to look for my son. He is so impulsive, you know.'

He rose and dashed out of the room, slamming the door behind him.

'Lanz . . . Lanz . . .'

She followed him into her room, very upset. They eyed one another maliciously, like hostile birds of prey. These two, who slept on top of each other, were strangers.

'Lanz, what do you want from me?'

He did not speak. He stood by the window, tense and angry, running his tapered dancer's fingers up and down the curtains.

'Lanz, I think about my son because he belongs to me. I love him.'

She stopped short, craning her slim neck. The noise she heard was like that of a table being knocked over. She recognized the sound of Patrice's footsteps when he was angry. Yes, Patrice had come home. He strode into the room with violence in his eyes, his clothes torn. He stared at the speechless couple, holding a whip in his hand, and the sight of a whip in his childlike fingers was strangely disturbing.

'My baby, where have you been?'

Patrice remembered that when Louise lived alone in this room she used to say, 'My baby, where have you been?' But her voice had never been so weak, so strangely cowed.

'Look at that big boy all covered with mud,' she tittered. But her laughter was brief, with a ring of terror.

'Put that whip down,' ordered Lanz, laying his gold cane on the child's arm.

Patrice had no intention of using the whip. He had come into the room meek and crushed, with a thirst which he did not know how to quench. But when he looked at the gold cane vibrating along his arm, he went wild. He raised his arms, as though suffocating. He wanted to shout, to cry, but the sounds caught in his throat. He held his breath, then his eyes fell on the cane again. A fearful desire came over him to break everything in this room, just as he had strewn the floor with fragments of glass, the night of the party.

'Patrice, why are you so pale?'

'Out of the room, Patrice!'

'Patrice, my baby . . .'

'I said out, Patrice.'

Suddenly, Patrice struck Lanz's arm and sent the gold cane flying through the air. Unable to control the fury which took possession of him, he whipped the large male body that stood between him and his mother. Lanz leapt upon him and grabbed the whip. Patrice did not struggle. Lanz held him to the wall, pinning the delicate nape beneath his elbow. Patrice howled, the way he howled when he was delirious. Louise was frozen with shock.

'Lanz, Lanz, why?'

Blinded, with Louise's beloved child finally at his mercy, Lanz began to whip him. After several blows, he sighed and shrugged his shoulders.

'I am your father, Patrice. Don't forget that. I am taking his place. Now you can go.'

Louise was relieved to see that he had not touched the boy's face, that only his shoulders were red. She threw herself upon her son. Patrice sobbed, leaning against her.

*

TWO

1

Patrice
roamed
the forest
the rest
of the night.

He walked without dreaming, without thinking, without living, and yet he still trembled from the shock, like a man who has been saved from drowning but who still battles the ocean within himself. He wandered on and on through the underbrush, swinging his arms from the shoulder like an acrobat.

A storm was brewing in the sky and the air was warmer. Two young bodies suddenly crossed through the trees like a falling star . . . Apprehension came over Patrice's face. He lay flat on the ground, his heart pounding. He recognized his sister's voice and another boyish voice, barely a man's, which laughed as soon as she stopped talking. Patrice hid his head beneath a pile of leaves and made swimming motions with his arms.

'Isabelle-Marie,' he murmured, 'Isabelle . . .'

She laughed. He had never heard her laugh so spontaneously. At home, Isabelle-Marie's laughter was deadening. Tonight it was enchanting. Patrice bit into some bark and tore it to pieces with his teeth. This act of biting calmed him.

He lay stretched out in the night. A bird cried and no voice answered. The bird flew away, glancing gently against Patrice's arm like a woman's lips. Patrice thought of the lake where he could cool his brow but it was too far away. He felt sick. Soon dawn would waken a purple world, mixing whiteness with the shadows. One could already smell the hay in the open barnyards. Patrice rolled from one side to the other. A beatific smile came over his face as he lay with one hand beneath his cheek. He was breathing fast.

'Isabelle-Marie, haven't you seen your brother?'

'No, Mother.'

Louise did not dare go into her daughter's room. Against the pink nightgown she was wearing, her face was horribly white, like someone's face after a severe shock. Disease hollowed her cheek.

'Why are you laughing, Isabelle-Marie?'

'I'm not supposed to laugh, am I?'

There was anguish in her mother's voice. 'Isabelle, I am very worried about Patrice. What is happening to him? Is it because I married Lanz?'

Isabelle-Marie, seated in front of her mirror, seemed to be sneering from the very depths of her soul. The sight of her was cold and eerie, like a gumless witch.

'What were you doing outside tonight?'

'Nothing, Mother.'

Louise's stern features expressed the hatred and contempt she bore for her daugher. She placed an icy hand on Isabelle-Marie's emaciated shoulder.

'Don't lie to me. You were not here tonight, and Lanz told me you have been doing very little on the farm these days.'

Isabelle-Marie tossed her hair back over her shoulders.

She gazed at this woman who was her mother, looking to see where her wound began, following it from its source as it drove a furrow of pain toward her temple, where her eyes fluttered with subtle perversity.

If only Louise had dared to love her daughter. Had Isabelle-Marie been a more simple creature, she might have grown up without malice. She had become embittered because of the passions that seethed within her. Wickedness was her second self; she was like those beings who lead two separate lives, one by day, and a more sinister one by night.

Louise, alas, had aged considerably during the last few days. All she needs to do now is grow old, thought Isabelle-Marie.

'Poor Lanz,' cried the young girl.

"He is my husband.'

'Yes, Mother, and you will be sorry.'

Louise's hand clutched the frail shoulder. Her nails pierced the skin. All her contempt for her daughter spurted like pus from her fingernails.

'Where were you tonight?'

'My dog was sick. I had to take care of him.'

'You are lying.'

Louise ripped her hand away from her daughter's shoulder, away from this flesh of her flesh. Then, still nervous and tense, she left the room. She wandered throughout the house, calling, 'Patrice . . . Patrice . . .' Finally she went back to her room where Lanz was waiting for her, fast asleep. Stopping on the threshold, she experienced for the first time a kind of shame, at herself, and at this man, as though he were something she had found lurking beneath her own skin. Lanz still wore a nasty smile. Half the shadows in the room had faded as day began to dawn. The light, breaking through the blinds, cast a black and white keyboard across the bed. With his gold cane still hanging on his arm, Lanz sighed in his sleep and his tapered fingers waltzed to the rhythm of his breathing.

He had fallen asleep still posing as a man of fashion. He thought, drank, ate, and slept in this role. It was a challenging game and he played it with consummate skill, like a secret vice which possessed his being. Lanz, whose nails were always manicured and whose shoes were always polished, had fallen asleep fully dressed, in all his offensive perfection.

Confronted with this, her own image, Louise squirmed in disgust. She leaned over to undress him, and from his mouth she inhaled her own breath. Feeling faint, she stood up and rubbed oil on her neck, trying to distract herself.

How odd, my pupils are dilated. Probably the anxiety.

The vulgar doll was trembling.

And your cheek? What have you there?

The blemish on her cheek was like a welt on a leper, a sinister patch which threatened to destroy her. She covered it with cream but the cream turned purple.

Now Patrice is all I have left. I don't love Lanz any more.

In truth she had never loved him. Now that he knew all her charms, she had no way of pleasing him.

But her soul cried within her, At least I can still count on him.

And, in her wild optimism, Patrice is beautiful. I have Patrice.

She slipped a raincoat over her shoulders, loosened her hair, and went out toward the woods. The rain was coming down very hard. As it streamed over her, the water wove a cloak of misery around her long body.

'Patrice! Patrice!'

She discovered her son lying on the forest floor. She shook him, wild with desperation.

'Patrice, my baby.'

He opened his eyes and his face seemed to bloom beneath his tears.

'You should be more careful,' she said, in a tender, faltering voice, 'especially after your fever.'

Patrice clung to her, begging her to protect him. His

words came so fast that she could not understand. He said that he was afraid, that he wanted to die.

'Patrice, what are you saying? Lanz never meant to hurt you.'

She put her coat around him. For a moment she stood looking at her son's face. All I have is this child, this face . . . only this face . . . Her heart burst with loneliness.

They went home in silence. A pall of sleep hung over the house.

2

Meanwhile, Isabelle was slowly coming to life in her love for Michael, her only chance to live and die. Love had, in a sense, turned her ugliness into an odd kind of beauty. She held roses between her teeth and was less bitter about her puny legs. She and Michael ran down the mountainside, wild with laughter. Isabelle-Marie would stumble so that Michael had to carry her, so that she could feel herself rocked by those strong arms, those oars of living flesh.

'Don't you know where we are going? It doesn't matter. There are two squirrels on our left. Listen . . .'

She looked.

'Why yes, two squirrels. You can sense everything.'

He was happy to know that Isabelle-Marie was so unique, so beautiful, especially when he held her close. He bit her neck and was thrilled by her virgin laughter.

'Tell me again that you are beautiful. I want you to be beautiful so much.'

'I am beautiful. I am beautiful.'

'Why are you trembling all of a sudden?'

'It's nothing. Just let me walk now.'

'What about your ankle? You told me you'd hurt it.'

'That was only to scare you.'

He obeyed and allowed the young girl to lead him by the hand.

'Shall we get married?'

'Crazy boy! You are not even twenty and with that snow-white hair you are a child, not a husband.'

Michael lifted his face toward the sky, which to him was dark and closed. He took a deep breath and his face wore the intensity of a seer.

'Is the world beautiful?'

'When it wishes to be beautiful.'

'But I know it is beautiful! I can listen to it. It smells so delicious.'

He gamboled and caressed Isabelle-Marie's hair which he believed was blond because it was so soft.

'This is where the men hunted for partridge.'

'Yes, right here. Yesterday.'

He had reconstructed the outside world within himself. He could describe a daisy better than someone who could see to strip its petals.

'These are white because everything that is delicate is white, and there is gold in the middle.'

'Yes, Michael, gold in the middle. You are right.'

He was wild and passionate, blessed with the same burning joys as a child. His blindness cloistered his existence but he spoke so knowingly of the life of animals, of the wind, and of the seasons, that one could only marvel at his insight. Isabelle-Marie loved him. She prayed that she could love him without hurting him. Growing up so near to each other, they thought neither of the flesh, nor of desire. Running and playing together was enough. Nevertheless, great struggles lay ahead. The day would come when the body arises, impelled by such overriding desire that reason itself is left behind, inert and silent. The children waited for that day, laughing.

'Isabelle, Isabelle, I want to drink at the spring.'

'First you must tell me what kind of a day it is and what color the sky is,' insisted Isabelle-Marie as she rubbed her wrist against the young man's hand.

He listened and meditated, and his eyes were wide open and beautiful.

'The sun is very warm and the sky is a fatal blue.'

'A fatal blue?'

She laughed.

'What an idea! You win. I will give you the whole spring to drink from.'

He licked his lips with pleasure.

'Will you also let me drink out of your hands?'

They ran together to the spring. He leaned over and his handsome white head rippled the water like the head of an angelic old man.

'You are drinking too much.'

'Oh, please, a little more.'

He submerged his whole face in the limpid water and then stretched, smelling pleasantly of hay. This morning he looked at Isabelle-Marie in an unusual way and she became worried.

'What are you thinking about, Michael?'

'Soon I shall able to see you. I can sense it.'

Isabelle-Marie dried his face and buried his head in her lap. I am forgetting Patrice, she thought.

'Isabelle!'

Michael suddenly uttered her name as though he needed to shout. The sound of his voice reminded Isabelle-Marie of the sad cries which came from her mother's room when Lanz was with her. She felt a chill.

'I want to go home, Michael.'

'Isabelle, Isa the Beautiful.'

He squeezed her arm with one hand and her waist with the other. The fingers which were trying to devour her waist-line were very warm.

'What is it you want?'

She escaped, but the boy grew excited and grabbed her again, and she fell on her knees before him. She felt a shortness of breath and a strange desire to cry, to lament all the emptiness of the world.

'Michael, what do you want? Tell me.'

She spoke quickly, trying to fend off a flood of protest.

'There are so many games we can play. I shall be a deer, like yesterday, and you must find out what I am saying, or else a bird . . . or else . . . I know, I shall pretend to be a swan and you must try to imagine me inside your heart.'

He was deaf. Suddenly he began to embrace her again.

'But what is the matter, Michael? Yesterday we had such a good time together. Today you are so different. Why, Michael, why?'

He sighed.

'I wish I knew.'

He leaned over Isabelle-Marie's neck, a gesture which he often repeated. But this time he leaned over as though to bite her.

'You are hurting me.'

Then the boy spoke like a man and his whole face changed.

'What I want is to have you against my heart, lying over me.'

'Hush.'

'It is you that I want.'

She rose, trying to flee, but he caught her and the bones in his feverish hand crackled.

'Come, lay your body beside mine, Isabelle-Marie. Lie over me, please. I desire you.'

She stiffened, and wept, holding her arm to her cheek.

He kissed her quickly on the nape of her neck.

'Don't you want to be mine?'

She did not answer.

'Isabelle, I am a farmer. I am as simple as the sand, but I love you. I won't do you any harm.'

She looked all around and bit her lips as if to rejoice and punish herself at the same time.

'The cats followed me again,' she said. 'Oh, if you could see them tumbling in the flowers, scratching each other.'

'Isabelle-Marie, come . . . please come . . .'

She did not answer.

'You seem to be crying.'

He ran his fingers down the length of her trembling cheek.

'Yes, you are crying.'

'No,' she said quickly, her pride stung. 'It is water from the spring.'

'The water from the spring is not so salty.'

'I want to go home. My brother is sick . . . and . . .'

He held her against the tree with all his might.

'Marry me tomorrow.'

'Yes, tomorrow.'

'I will give you the little house by the lake.'

'I will give you my body.'

She laughed through her tears. Then, in the end, she began to sob, abandoning herself upon his bare shoulder. She sensed that their 'games' were over. From now on everything would be very serious. Everything would be like Louise, like Lanz, like the vast tragedy in which they all were grave performers. She bit Michael's shoulder and he trembled.

He started to drink again, kneeling by the spring and swallowing the water with unquenchable delight, with the thirst of a twenty-year-old.

She kissed him on the nose. It was noon. They shared handfuls of fruit like kisses and thrilled to the song of the birds. Then they dipped their bread in the cool water.

The gentle feast was coming to an end.

4

The next day the Livanis gave a party at the farm for the newlyweds. There was dancing until dawn. Louise was overjoyed to be losing her daughter. As she helped her to dress, hypocrisy masked her delight at being so easily rid of the sharp-eyed scrutiny of Isabelle-Marie, her monstrous virgin daughter. Once married, Isabelle-Marie would become silent, body and soul. So she encouraged her, and Lanz, too, rejoiced inwardly to see this annoying critic disappear from their lives.

'In a little while, Isabelle-Marie,' Michael was saying, 'I shall see you.'

She shivered.

After fervent vows and a ceremony full of laughter as poignant as a cheerful farewell, the bride and groom went back to the spring. From there they could hear the singing of the Livani children, of that whole immense and close-knit family. They played their old games again, Isabelle-Marie trying to outdistance Michael as he became more lithe and animated in pursuit of this flesh which he could not see.

'The song you can hear is a whitethroat. And listen! The little squirrel with the white tail is about to jump.'

'Who said its tail is white?'

'I say so.'

He lay down, half upon her, his head resting on her belly. His eyes widened. Their black, adolescent depths were as inviting as two mouths. The children went on with their games until midnight.

'Now it is completely dark,' said Michael, opening his arms.

He knew when night had fallen. Large pale birds came

together above the warm lake and then lit on the shore. Michael shook his fragrant curls and laughed, 'Other birds have forgotten to sleep after sunset.'

At that moment the creatures of the forest were busier than ever. They gathered together and keened, to make their presence known. Isabelle-Marie and Michael, with their knees joined, remembered somewhat anxiously that they had been consecrated as 'man and wife' that morning.

That night he did not have to accompany her to the house where Louise and Lanz whiled away their time in the lamplight, where Patrice stared at the wall with a nostalgia that was so distant, so mysterious that no one could understand its meaning: the melancholy of a man who does not know why.

They walked in silence.

Meanwhile, Patrice, angry at everything—at Louise who was no longer, since the arrival of her gigolo, 'his own Louise's —stamped his feet in wild rage. He had not forgotten Lanz's whipping. The scene came back in his dreams, grotesque and painful. Except when he haunted the woods with the horses, Patrice lived alone in his room, in front of his mirrors. But he was growing weary of himself. His own features no longer gave him pleasure.

Ever since he was a child, Patrice had imitated his mother. Louise used a great deal of make-up. So he, too, began to play with the dazzling colors. One morning he awoke with the idea of making his face into a devil's mask and disfigured his cheeks as he tried to achieve the right expression. This new game helped him pass the time alone. But he soon grew tired of it. He lost interest in everything but his horses. Physical violence took possession of him and gave him the fantastic speed and prowess of a giant. But he took dangerous risks; he almost collapsed the sides of his horse. Louise did not know what to say to him any more and was afraid. In spite of her devotion to Lanz, the sterile adversary with whom she slept, deep within herself she was in constant anguish at the thought of losing Patrice, whose overwhelming beauty still kept a hold over her. When she came home, at night or at dawn, she did not look at her son's hands, or his chest, but at his face. The slightest marring of his face would have stricken her instantly with terror.

'Lanz, is Patrice in his room?'

Lanz answered, in his flat jesting voice which had so little resonance, "Yes, he is in there. I hear glass breaking.'

Louise ran into the room. The ribbon around her head broke suddenly, and her hair tumbled down.

'Oh, Patrice, my baby! You broke the mirror.'

Patrice wandered through Isabelle-Marie's and Michael's new house. At least Isabelle-Marie still called him 'My Beautiful, Beautiful Beast' and caressed his head. At least Isabelle-Marie was aware of his existence. He had entered their house without a sound, in his bare feet, his clothes covered with spots. Whenever Isabelle-Marie saw him disheveled like this, she always promised him clean, warm clothes, and now he waited naïvely, like a child waiting for a miracle.

A low roar could be heard across the lake. The lamps dimmed and cast a thin beam, like a large illuminated vein, across the loaf of fresh bread, the flowers from the night before, and the two glasses of champagne. Patrice paused to enjoy the tingling sensation in his bare feet. Alert and tense, the muscles of his face quivered beneath the skin. In his innocent games he had grown tall; blond down was appearing on his chin and his cheeks, and one wondered, looking at him, how such a child could become a man.

Patrice enjoyed feeling the bare floor beneath his heels. It made him shiver. Every physical stimulus made him feverish with excitement. He laughed into his hands, to calm himself. The aroma of the champagne left in the glasses and the fragrance of the fresh white bread filled him with satisfaction. He was approaching the bridal chamber. He murmured, 'Isabelle-Marie, Isabelle-Marie.'

Standing very still in front of the door which he hesitated to open, he thought of his mother's room. The clock struck twice, with a slow, grating noise. He went in. The darkness within the room suddenly made him thirsty.

The bride and groom were asleep. Michael's foot lay peacefully across the white folds of the sheet. Patrice clung to the wall. Everything in his mind began to spin: the whip, Lanz's hand, his gloves, the bread which Isabelle-Marie had hidden from him, his face, the water.

He sighed, thinking he was dreaming, the way a drowning man dreams that he really is not dying. Isabelle-Marie and Michael must have struggled physically for a long time to sleep so profoundly. The most rare and precious sleep there is! Their clothes and some straw hats that were still warm were strewn around the room. Michael slept half turned on his side and the whiteness of the sheets outlined his ardent, tanned young body. They held hands as they slept, as though ready to rise, to go back to their games in the mist or on the mountainside. Only their heads lay side by side and united, slipping closer together now and then as they rose and fell to the same rhythm.

'Isabelle-Marie, I have hurt myself. I have hurt my knee.

Patrice was timidly pleading with a person who no longer knew he was alive.

The children slept. Patrice grew tired, stroking his knee with a vague gesture. He could hear Isabelle-Marie's breathing and, above it, that of Michael. Why was he trembling? Was it because the disorder in the room reminded him of the forest glades in the autumn?

Isabelle-Marie woke with a start. Her eyes widened and she lifted herself on one elbow.

'Patrice, what are you doing here?'

Patrice could not see her in the darkness. He had startled her in the midst of a nightmare. Suddenly he grew afraid of his sister and left. The woods comforted him and he forgot his bitterness. But he could not sleep. His knee ached sharply and he pressed it with his nails or against his cheek. He was no longer delirious. A few feet away some cats were fighting, shrieking their terrible love to one another. Raucous moaning shook them from within, pitiless as a death rattle. The male clutched the female and the look in his huge tortured eyes changed from animal to human, and from human to an expression of morbid, inexorable desire. Patrice's eyes were the same green, but untroubled. He watched this fearful battle of instincts, these collisions of the flesh, and listened anxiously to this chorus of laments. He could not intervene and save the female from the weight of all those claws, because she wanted the embraces and the biting of the male before abandoning herself to him. She needed these wounds in order to savor the pleasures to come, pleasures that would be all the more excruciating. What bestial will power! What savage, secret endurance! Would these cats enjoy the same deep sleep that he had seen on the faces of Michael and Isabelle-Marie?

Patrice shuddered, without understanding. He sensed vaguely that he was of the same race as these 'beautiful beasts.' He bit the way they did and moaned the way they did, because he did not know how to express himself as a man, and he drove himself when he ran with the stubborn strength of an animal.

Finally the female surrendered.

Patrice foundered within himself, in the hollow depths of his being.

5

Once again the chess game brought Louise and Lanz beneath the lamplight. Louise was using more and more make-up, trying to hide the scandalous vein on her cheek. She was still absorbed in her own frivolity, while Lanz, with his opaque heart and his eyes that were like those of a bat, continued his monotonous and elegant existence. Patrice, who feared those eyes, stayed alone in his room, daydreaming.

Louise longed to return to this beloved, ill-loved son but she feared that he saw through her hypocrisy. She was more and more afraid of his opinion of her. Patrice, however, though she was still unaware of it, had no opinions.

'Eat a little bread,' said Louise to Patrice. 'You haven't eaten since yesterday.'

But he was not listening and his mute face turned away from her. Then he cut the bread himself, piercing the doughy core with his thumb.

'Patrice, cut some bread for Lanz.'

Lanz and his gold cane were still inseparable. It made him look like a rich angel, lent him an aura of nobility, an illusion of freedom.

'Patrice, darling, please!'

When they sat together at meals, Patrice tortured his mother without knowing it. She blushed and trembled as she ate. I must never lose Patrice, she thought. I must never lose his beauty.

Lanz looked at her with an icy, reproachful stare. She smiled; they both smiled, but simultaneously, as though with a single mouth. Isabelle-Marie's place was empty. Louise unconsciously offered her some bread.

'Isabelle-Marie,' she pleaded, in her distraction, suddenly seeing her daughter before her as of old, brandishing a knife as though to rip her to pieces.

She grew silent, her long fingers touching her lips. The faintest appeal to her coquetry, however, was enough to free Louise from her worries. Lanz was merry and lavished jewels upon her, for a great many jewels and thick make-up were necessary to disguise the viper that crept along her cheek. Her delicate wrist was always richly adorned, as was her throat. Now she wore a choker to hide her wrinkles.

Patrice left before the meal was over. The moment he was outside, flies clung to his skin and stung him.

He walked without noticing, a forgotten Adonis.

He mounted his horse, breathing deeply. His arms were bronze and muscular, his back strong and virile, and his beautiful mouth was open, showing his teeth that sparkled as though a woman's tear glistened on each one. A man? A child among men? Indefinable in the midst of infinity? Unpredictable in the midst of chance? A free man who knew neither the origins of his freedom nor why he should use it? Would this melancholy god ride straight through the sunset that spread out before him like towers traced in red? He seemed capable of anything. And yet the spirit within him was feeble, timorous, overawed—and profoundly empty.

A partridge darted behind a rock; another, of a different color, flew to join the first, and then there was silence. Standing in the luxuriant grass, the horse grew restless; its mane rose stiffly, and as the fragrance of the wheat tickled its nostrils it stamped impatiently. Finally it set off with Patrice crouched low on its neck.

'Faster! Faster!'

Crushed by the galloping hooves, juicy strawberries spurted scarlet against the breast of the frenzied beast.

The branches which hung across the path whipped Patrice's back and a new madness took possession of him. His eyes became as wild as an animal's; he bit his lips until

73

he cried. This weeping horseman, as unharnessed as his mount, laid waste to everything he passed.

Patrice abandoned himself to speed, desperately trying to discover the person he might have become. He had a wild craving for mirrors . . . He grew so intoxicated that had his horse, with no hand to guide it, carried him headlong into the lake, he would not have struggled or wondered why. Suddenly, out of the corner of his eye, he thought he saw Louise and Lanz in a tight embrace, fleeing into the bushes.

'Faster! Faster!'

The horse, also drunk with speed, raced harder, straining against the ultimate limits of its strength. Yes. To race, and race, and die at the finish line, in the heat of passion.

Louise, horrified, watched the horse bear down upon Lanz. She tried to grab his arm but instead drew only the gold cane to her side. Lanz, stunned by the ghastly vision that threatened, drew back and yelled, losing, in that instant all his lordly veneer.

Louise shouted, 'Stop, Patrice, stop!'

These last cries spread out like waves upon the air. Near by, the spring gushed live and clear. Louise collapsed. Lanz was knocked down. He lay inert and lifeless, stretched out near the spring, his chest crushed, while the dazed horse disappeared into the distance, leaving Patrice near the victim.

Patrice rose and burst into an inane kind of laughter, a laughter that had a tragic ring in this vast, deathly silence. Standing speechless by her husband, Louise could not breathe; this time she was genuinely stricken.

Lanz moaned, 'Louise, Patrice, I'm afraid to die.'

Half prostrate, his head whirling, Patrice could not see anything.

He was staring into an idiot's blue void.

The dull voice continued to murmur, 'Patrice, I don't want to die.'

6

How could such an empty being die? Lanz felt himself growing cold, he who had never thought of death nor of the death of the spirit, he whose gods were his clothes, his women, Louise's jewels, and a gold cane.

Bleeding heavily, the elegant Lanz longed to weep.

'I don't want to die,' he kept repeating, covered with mud and sweat.

One outstretched hand clutched the gold cane, as the blood ran from his body. But the cane was carried away in the stream, like a veil from last night's ball.

His dying voice repeated, 'Patrice . . .'

As though a stranger in this tragedy which had started as a game, Patrice watched the gold cane disappear like a melting sword, and also, something which no one had yet noticed, Lanz's wig as it parted from his scalp. Moreover, saturated with blood, Lanz's false beard was falling apart.

He was decomposing before he died.

Louise fell upon him, cradling his head between her hands, caring for his wounds with a grave and trembling hand, a hand that was at last human. Louise's hands, though beautiful, were rarely 'human.'

She cried and cried. When she lifted her face, battered with sobs, she understood that Lanz was dead. She looked at Patrice, first vindictively, then with an anguished expression which said, 'Patrice, you are all I have left.'

Just at that moment the sun let loose its torrential fires over the whole forest, for it, too, was dying.

Lanz, who had always maintained a splendid appearance, now slept naked and exposed. Patrice no longer saw the gold cane.

After this tragedy, Patrice retreated into a sullen, childish silence. Louise, dressed in black, did not go to the woods any more. Often she spent the whole night sitting in front of the chessboard, while the lamps, which recalled the gesturing ghost of Lanz, kept vigil.

But soon her vanity came to life again. She clung more than ever to the presence of her son. She spoke to him and he did not seem to hear her. She questioned him about his racing and the plant life which he loved to watch. Within his body Patrice was asleep. After all kinds of wiles and caresses she would finally hold his adolescent face between her hands, saying, with slight fear in her voice, 'Patrice, don't you recognize your mother?'

Little by little, the spell of her soothing words won him back. He 'rested' his head in its former sanctuary, the hollow of Louise's shoulder, and remained there without moving, his closed eyes hiding an idiot's secrets.

'Why did you want to kill my husband, Patrice? I saw you, you know . . . You dug your heels into the animal's sides until you drove him into a frenzy.'

Actually Patrice did not remember, or remembered only vaguely, the horse's flowing mane, his swollen, aching knee, the gold cane, and the wig, yes . . . the wig.

Everything grew confused. His idiot's memory was like an empty box in which the mechanisms of remorse were out of order and which was no more resilient than the heart of a madman.

'Patrice, don't try to hide anything from me; I can read it in your eyes. I have always been able to read your eyes. Tell me, you wanted to kill Lanz for a long time, didn't you?'

Even when she said this, there was little vengeance in her voice. She stroked Patrice's blond head with her fingers. She was bitter but she managed a woeful smile. The vein disfigured her cheek more and more and one could tell, by looking at her weary eyelids, that she cried a great deal during the night.

'You are unreasonable, Patrice, really you are. You wanted me to yourself, didn't you? But why did you have to make me suffer?'

He murmured into her bosom, 'Run, run . . . keep running!'

She nestled Patrice against her shoulder. He was like a drowning man looking for dry ground.

'No one will ever find out that you killed Lanz. Even I will forget.'

Instead of giving her relief, the tears burned her cheek. Tears always overwhelmed Patrice, especially his mother's. He could not endure them.

He almost smothered her as he sobbed, 'Don't cry. I won't let you cry.'

But he did not know what he was saying. The tears, the mystery of this shoulder which protected him, the warm arms around his head, this whole embrace made him dizzy. Loved and hated at once, he buried himself deeper against her.

'Mother, I won't let you cry.'

Louise blinked and said nothing.

7

The news of Lanz's death was no shock to Isabelle-Marie. She had hated him so much, the odious creature who hung around her mother's neck, the male replica of this live mannequin. Now she was happy. Isabelle-Marie was no longer insecure; she did not doubt her make-believe beauty. She no longer had to repeat, 'I have violet eyes.' She believed it. Eager lies often turn into a kind of faith. She devoted herself to discovering the body and soul of her husband, laughing with him, encouraging his youthful passion. She lived her dream without weakness, rejoicing in every moment of it.

'Michael, are you asleep? It's time to get up! I want to pick cherries with you this morning.'

'It's sunny today, isn't it?' asked Michael as he stretched. 'My leg is very warm.'

The naïve joys which they shared drew them close together in the flesh and in the spirit. They rediscovered each other again and again in childish innocence and did not believe that they could ever be separated. As they awakened to the excitement of desire, they promised and gave everything to one another, eyes, arms, loins, everything.

'Get up, Michael!'

She laughed against his chest, kissing him.

'Someday I will have children, Michael. But don't worry, I will have enough love for you and for them, too.'

'Is my Isa beautiful today?'

'Dazzling.'

He breathed the fragrance of her hair, rose, dressed carelessly, and then, still half-naked, ran with her along the shore of the lake. They slipped their fishing boat gently into the water and when they came home in the evening, they were as weatherbeaten and disheveled as two old salts. They smelled of fish and algae, and they were singing lustily.

Michael, who thought very little about his infirmity, bloomed with the grace of a young god. For the two of them, living together meant living in one another, playing 'games.'

Isabelle-Marie listened to the soul of her brother-husband, her child-brother, this tall young man who not so long before used to wander barefoot in the mountains, cutting himself arrows from the branches of trees. His natural intuition astonished others and even astonished himself.

Peace and candor reigned within him.

One morning when Isabelle-Marie had gone hunting with her husband, she saw him bend down with one knee raised, over which he spread the wings of a butterfly.

'Michael, one doesn't kill butterflies.'

She remembered that the night of the ball she had told him, 'One doesn't kill spiders.' And he had resented it.

'I'll kill what I feel like killing,'' said Michael.

In this brutal and selfish gesture, Isabelle-Marie found something of herself—herself as she had been when she hid the bread from her brother. Suddenly very disturbed, she bit her husband's hand. The butterfly flew away by itself, toward the sun.

Michael was shocked and leaned forward as if to curse her, but she begged him to be more gentle.

'Michael, my beloved, have you forgotten how beautiful I am?'

She went on caressing him to calm his anger.

'We will have to cut your nails,' she said coyly.

But he had risen to his feet and was walking around, bumping into everything.

'Michael, listen to me, listen, I have a surprise for you.'

Michael's bare feet trampled the grass.

'Michael . . .'

Suddenly Isabelle-Marie's face was transfigured. If Michael could have seen his wife then, radiant with joy, he would have admired her in one of her rare moments of beauty.

'Michael, I am going to be a mother. I will bear a child as handsome as you.'

Forgetting his anger, he kissed the hem of her dress.

Then he asked, naïvely happy, 'And why not as beautiful as you?' He was bursting with joy. 'Yes, with violet eyes, and his mouth . . . What is your mouth like, Isa?'

'Like a delicate basket between my cheeks. You told me so, the night of our wedding.'

8

Michael, whom sleep had tossed against his wife's back, woke up murmuring into Isabelle-Marie's hair, 'Isabelle-Marie, our little girl is crying.'

She closed his lips with her thin hand and breathed peacefully beside him, while the child continued to cry nearby.

'Isabelle-Marie, our baby may be sick.'

Half-asleep, Isabelle-Marie rose, found a candle, rocked the child, and then, when the baby girl did not stop crying, she took her in her arms and hugged the fragile little head against her cheek, humming a tune. Michael leaned toward them.

'What is it?'

'Only a fever.'

'Your daughter is beautiful, isn't she?'

'Yes, like you.'

But she looked like Isabelle-Marie. From the day of her birth Isabelle-Marie had found the baby even more hideous than herself, and the tiny face, afflicted by the same ugliness, bearing her blood and the same tortured features, repelled her.

'I wonder why she has that birthmark on her left temple.'

'What did you say?'

She did not answer and Michael went back to sleep.

It was raining. They had forgotten to tie up the boat. As the waters of the lake rose and fell, it floated away.

Michael trembled in his sleep.

Isabelle-Marie, mortified, wished she could die so that she would not have to suffer because of her daughter.

Meanwhile, Michael, his body as lithe as a woodcutter's, continued to tremble, as though he were swimming beneath the sheets.

Isabelle-Marie felt the child's mouth trying to return to her breast. The child cried. She closed the blinds.

Michael, still in bed, was pinching the corners of his eyelids.

'Is something wrong, Michael? What is the matter with your eyes?'

He rubbed his eyelids with his fists and Isabelle-Marie was afraid. She clung to her child.

"Michael, get up now! We are going fishing.'

He tossed on the bed for a few minutes, as though delirious. The lower part of his face was harder than marble.

'Michael, open your eyes, Michael.'

Michael opened his eyes. They grew wider and wider and from the way he was looking at her, Isabelle-Marie knew that he could see. She was instantly ashamed. She backed up against the wall with her hands clutching her throat as though to strangle herself. Michael stood up with his hands outstretched. His eyes focused on Isabelle with weird intensity.

'Isabelle-Marie, is it possible? Were you lying? Please tell me that my eyes are deceiving me.'

She was sobbing. He came nearer and grabbed, and then dropped, her thin hands. He looked at her piercingly, for a long time, while she stood before him, rigid and white with anger.

'So you are really ugly, Isabelle-Marie?'

She looked as though she were about to faint, and her face quivered with suffering.

'Yes, I am ugly.'

Wild with despair, shrinking in horror from the one whom he had loved so much when she was 'beautiful,' he shrieked, 'Liar! Liar!'

She answered in a low voice, without stirring, 'It is a

miracle that you are able to see, Michael. It was also a miracle that made me beautiful.'

He came back to his wife's side and began to strike her across the face. It was as though they had never slept next to one another. She remained silent and did not flinch, for the blows brought back her former toughness and endurance. She knew that she was stronger than he.

'Michael, go away. What are you waiting for?'

As if in defiance, she offered him her bleeding face, with its black eyes, blacker than ever through her tears.

'Go away.'

But Michael, who was still fingering his eyelids, fell on his knees and cried into her skirt. Afterwards, he left without looking at her.

The child was crying. But Isabelle-Marie had suffered such an immense and lacerating wound that she could not hear.

She dressed the child quickly and went home to her mother. She was of the race of the ugly, destined to be scorned. For her there was only one refuge, one place in the world that could offer her welcome: the earth. When she entered the house, with the child beneath her torn coat and her face like a wasteland where the Terror had passed, she felt a need to vomit. Perverse desires ached in her heart.

Louise moved away from her solitary chess game.

'Isabelle-Marie! Did you come to show me your baby girl?'

Isabelle-Marie hid the child and disappeared into her room.

Patrice sat in a corner, manicuring his nails like a girl.

Days and days went by. Isabelle-Marie never smiled and her pitiful self-control gradually hardened her.

She lived in the fields, in the stable, taking care of the animals and talking very little. Before her stood Patrice, always Patrice, the one who was admired, understood, the Idiot! The uglier she felt, the more crushed and humiliated, the more she thought about destroying her brother's unjust beauty.

Patrice had forgotten almost all his sorrows and was content in his new security. His mother again welcomed him into her boudoir when she was brushing her hair. Once more she kept up her pointless monologue with this beloved, hollow creature.

All the sweetness which Lanz had taken away from him was now lavished again on Patrice. With it, the child rediscovered his love for himself, his confidence in the perfect harmony of his own body. He ate and drank and went walking with his mother.

He was noble and handsome. He was twenty years old.

*

THREE

*

1

Isabelle-Marie
had
been
sitting
by
the window for two hours, impassive and
motionless, her arms around her knees. A small vaporous
cloud wafted above the candle on the corner of the table.
She stared with savage intensity at everything that oppressed
her: the bread and water laid out for Patrice, the chessboard,
and the image of Louise waiting for her son night after night.
Even the roar of the fire in the hearth.

Isabelle-Marie dug her nails into her knees, seeking out
the most sensitive spots.

Louise rose and found herself near the lamp. The light
revealed the crawling sore on her cheek. Was she feverish?
She held one hand to her mouth and Isabelle-Marie saw that
she was trembling.

'It is very late, Isabelle-Marie. I hope Patrice is not on
the road.'

Isabelle-Marie did not answer. In spite of the fire, she was
shivering. Her chill was deep-seated, overpowering.

'Isabelle-Marie, I told him how dangerous it was to race the horses. When he hurt Lanz . . .'

'Patrice killed Lanz. It's not the same thing.'

Louise came over and sat down gloomily. Thinking that Isabelle-Marie would not notice, she rubbed her cheek with the back of her hand, to wipe away the pus.

'What could this be?' she muttered to herself in private terror. 'I thought that it was an ordinary bruise . . . but . . .'

Isabelle-Marie laughed scornfully. The sound pierced Louise's heart and reverberated through the empty house like the eerie footsteps of a supernatural visitor.

'What is wrong, Isabelle-Marie?'

Isabelle-Marie rose without answering.

'Isabelle-Marie!'

Patrice entered the room. He was now twenty-two and glowing with youth in every limb and fiber. His brow had never been so pure. He was panting with the cold; his scarves had come untied and flowed over his shoulders. He stretched out his arms and his mother came to embrace him.

'My darling, what were you doing? Come here, into the light. Tell me.'

'I was hunting.'

'Don't lie to me.'

She helped him take off his tall boots, boots which had belonged to her first husband.

'Wait a minute, let me wipe off your face. Promise me to rest; don't get up before dawn to run in the woods.'

'Yes, I would like to sleep.'

'Tell me what you were doing,' she pleaded as she buried her son's face in the pine-scented towels.

'I don't remember anything.'

'That is always your excuse,' she scolded. 'You don't want me to know. Would you like anything to drink? Isabelle-Marie has prepared some wine. And your bread . . . Eat something. But no, this bread is too fresh. What has come over

Isabelle-Marie, giving my baby bread still warm from the oven?'

Louise, thin and more attractive from a distance, moved away, poured some wine and came back to him smiling. Fear no longer lurked in her eyes. Her Beautiful Beast was there before her, her handsome, powerful, and empty-headed boy.

Patrice dozed off with his arm folded beneath his ruddy cheek. His eyelashes fluttered slightly, and a thin saliva, like the saliva of a child, glistened on his teeth.

Louise gazed at him in contentment. Patrice gave her everything she sought, for to him she was beautiful. This was her life. Her vanity had replaced Lanz with Patrice.

Patrice started, as though tormented by a dream. His breathing grew slower. He was buried deeper than ever in sleep, his own enduring sleep.

She led him to his room and put him to bed the way she had when he was still a child, helpless in the arms of his mother. Louise would spend some evenings punishing Isabelle-Marie, while Patrice fell asleep, lulled by affection.

She closed the blinds.

The pain in her cheek tightened like a vice.

'Tomorrow, yes tomorrow, I will see the doctors.'

But she knew that she would not go. She would rather wait. She lay down. Fever made her toss on her bed all night.

Autumn was coming to an end. Isabelle-Marie, close-mouthed, her soul withered, had worked too hard in the fields. She was growing thinner, uglier, as crabbed as an old witch; even her voice had changed. It was a voice without compassion, in which one could always sense a sneer.

One night she was walking her dogs in the woods. She liked being near her animals, with the miserably bare forest around her. That night a storm was brewing and the wind was bending everything low, but she walked bareheaded, scorning the elements. Gunshots rang out. Patrice must be playing, she thought. But one of the dogs grew scared and fled as though someone had called it. The shots rang out again, dull and repeated. She heard her dog moan. Only she could recognize that moaning.

'The youngest, he killed the youngest.'

She ran up, wild, black, and barefoot. Patrice was standing with the dead dog at his feet.

'What have you done, Patrice?'

At first he was startled, then he approached his sister.

'You killed my best dog.'

Patrice touched the dead dog without looking at it. Then, trying to console her, he stroked Isabelle-Marie's hair.

'You are an idiot, Patrice, a big idiot.'

Patrice, far away, empty-headed, and without identity, asked, 'Who? Me?'

She wrenched herself from him, crying 'Idiot!'

His face twisted in anguish, Patrice took refuge against a tree. His body reflected the same dread that had come over him years before, when Lanz had whipped him. He ran through the woods to the lake, where he leaned over and drank voraciously. The water was as icy as his sorrow.

'Patrice! Patrice!'

His sister was calling. Afraid, wanting to hide, Patrice tried to carry the watery image with him.

In spite of herself, Isabelle-Marie loved her daughter. She would rock the baby against her thin breast, feeling an intimate pleasure, the only pleasure she could call her own. But when she thought about what this child would become later on, an ugly duckling whom everyone would avoid, she was almost tempted to kill her.

Resentment of Patrice continued to gnaw at her. She watched him constantly and blamed him for everything. She felt contempt toward their mother who had never known how to divide her affection fairly between her children. Jealousy throbbed at her temples, like the consuming passion of the damned. She had to satisfy this passion or die.

The winter was hard. Patrice, loved and spoiled, stayed at home where he would not soil his clothes or break his beautiful nails. Isabelle-Marie spied on everything he did.

One morning when she woke up, Louise found pus on her neck and decided to consult the doctors about her 'scratch.'

When she came home, at the end of the day, Patrice was waiting for her. She was in tears and wore a dressing on her cheek.

'Mother,' asked Patrice as he kissed her, 'what is the matter?'

'Nothing, my darling. I was so cold. The cold always makes me cry. You know that. Are you looking at this bandage? It is nothing, Patrice dear, nothing. A bruise, it will heal very soon.'

She could say no more. Smiling at her son through her tears, she went to her room where she buried her face in her hands. Patrice did not understand.

Isabelle-Marie, who had been listening, laughed scornfully into her skirt.

Alone at last, Louise threw herself upon the bed, her arms clasped around her stomach.

Cancer! Cancer of the cheek!

Then she pulled herself together, did her make-up over, and removed the dressing.

'But it will not kill me.'

She smiled at the mask in the mirror which looked as though an axe had struck it across the right cheek.

'At least I have Patrice.'

Louise redid her make-up several times a day. In place of the dressing she applied warm, evil-smelling creams which changed the color of her skin. Age was hollowing her features, straining her neck and her brow. Only her hair was still elegant.

Isabelle-Marie stayed in her own room, next to the fire, or went walking in the forest with her daughter. She grew wan during this wan winter.

Forgetting her shameful disease in the presence of her son and encouraged by her vanity, Louise continued to believe in life.

But beneath her make-up she could often feel the pus oozing. Then she would bury her cheek in a handkerchief.

On some evenings, near the end of the season, Patrice found her depleted, nurturing some inward fury that in his innocence he could not understand. On the rare occasions when she played chess with Isabelle-Marie, she would let her daughter win and then retire early, saying she wanted to sleep. Once back in her room she would give in to pain, thrashing about on her bed like someone severely burned, spending long, arduous nights in which she suffered too much to sleep.

Patrice, who thought of her as a cherished sister, like his mirror or the reflection in the lake, Patrice who had such a desperate need to offer his beauty to someone, was baffled by these strange developments. Whenever he dared speak to Isabelle-Marie, she would laugh in his face. Then he would go back to Louise who would beg him never to abandon his mother for a girl friend or a wife.

'I am your mother, your best friend. I am part of you and you are part of me. Never forget that.'

He smiled and looked away while Louise shuddered in agony beneath her gaudy mask.

Spring came and the work began again in the fields. Every day at dawn Patrice scattered bread for the birds. As he spread his arms to divide it among them, he seemed like a saint in a medieval legend. He walked with his mother, his head always against her shoulder. Fires burned around them in the woods, whistling, as though born of the ice. Patrice noticed that his mother's shoulder was no longer as inviting nor as solid beneath his head. Louise would turn home very quickly, pretending that she was sleepy. The sinister worm gnawed into her cheek. When she laughed, one could see that she was suffering.

Louise had left a pan full of water on the fire. She was in the habit of using boiling water to soothe her cheek, now that her suffering had become worse. Today she sat transfixed by her mirror, sobbing quietly, her face eaten away from within. The fever would not go away. She forgot about the water boiling away in the pan. Isabelle-Marie stood with her elbows against the wall, her head thrown back and her lips drawn. As Patrice, carefree and handsome, walked back and forth in front of the hearth, Isabelle-Marie watched him, dreading his every step. She wanted to admire him for the last time.

Then she said in a very sad voice, 'My Beautiful Beast, lean over the flames. Watch them glow; you could gather them in your hands if you like.'

Patrice burst out laughing like a child, wonder filling his large, trusting eyes.

'Could I? Could I really play with the fire? Mother is afraid of fire.'

Isabelle-Marie crept closer and spoke without looking at him. Because she was stroking his shoulder and the nape of his neck, Patrice thought she was very sweet.

"Look, my Beautiful Beast. Lean over and touch them! You can gather them like stars.'

'Stars?' he asked, with a vacant expression.

She saw him standing there beside her, magnificent and calm. Such temptations must have possessed Eve as she prepared to seduce Adam. She hesitated, digging her teeth into the tenderest spot on her lip.

'Just lean over, my Beautiful Beast.'

Patrice stood stupidly in front of the water, which was beginning to boil over.

Driven by savage desires, Isabelle-Marie pursed her lips as if with curiosity.

'And now what do you see?'

'Water.'

'Why no, you must look more closely.'

A genius at injuring all those who did not suffer as she did, Isabelle-Marie dominated her brother, overcoming his resistance with a single glance.

'Why have you become so gentle with me all of a sudden?' Patrice ventured to ask.

She caressed him more ardently and as she did so she dug her nails into the nape of his neck, a man's neck beneath a child's bewildered face, fascinated by the flames.

'Such a beautiful, beautiful beast!'

Her malicious eyes focused on this gleaming nape. Her hand hesitated in midair and then, triumphant, it plunged Patrice's head into the boiling water. This hand was as strong as a claw and Patrice, who did not even cry out, was taken unawares as a human sacrifice. After her impulse had been satisfied, Isabelle-Marie went down the dark stairs leading to a part of the house which had been closed since the death of her father. There she stood, white and speechless, gasping for breath like someone with a bad heart.

Above, Patrice howled, beating his swollen face against anything in sight.

Isabelle-Marie heard her mother run up to him and burst into sobs. All hell broke loose above her head. Shaking off the deathly burden which had oppressed her for so long, Isabelle-Marie finally began to breathe freely.

Now at last there would be no more Beautiful Beast!

She pressed her hands to her cheeks, where the sweat ran like tears.

Louise looked at her disfigured son, without being able to throw herself upon him as a real mother would have done. She hid her face in her skirt. Her cheek bled over her hands.

'Patrice, don't make such horrible faces. Are you trying to scare me?'

She stood there biting her nails, unable to console the boy who stood before her, panting, his face as purple and shiny as a senile old man's.

'Patrice, what have you done?'

Patrice clawed at his mother's ankles, crying out in pain. But Louise pulled away from his clutches; she was not physically able to bear the sight of such a desperately injured being.

'Patrice, I told you to be careful, not to play near the fire.'

Neither her voice nor her words were the same. Violent egotism flared up within her. Patrice no longer meant anything to her, for her soul was that of a doll. With one slender foot she pushed away Patrice's forehead, the forehead she had once thought was like the breast of a swan. Overcome with disgust, she fled.

'It hurts, Mother, it hurts.'

'Isabelle-Marie, go take care of your brother,' Louise called in a dry tone of voice.

The silence surprised her.

'Isabelle-Marie, where are you?'

Isabelle-Marie appeared, a dull look in her eyes.

'Your brother has had an accident.'

Her voice faded suddenly, too gutteral to be human. She went back to her room, leaving her son wild with suffering.

He won't say anything, thought Isabelle-Marie. His stupidity will protect me.

She bore the poor child to his room, delighted to find him so ugly, to know that he would be plagued forever by this fiery wound. She listened to him as he blew on his arms and beat his fists against his chest.

'Well, my Beautiful Beast, what were we doing just then?'

Fortunately the water had spared Patrice's eyes. His eyelids were not bleeding but all the rest of his once-beautiful face was raw. Glimmers of real madness and terror came into his eyes.

'My Beautiful Beast, will you ever be sensible?'

Her brother tipped his head comically, his green eyes anxious and roving.

'You can calm down now, I am going to take care of you.'

'Mother . . . Mother . . .' he cried.

She had to struggle to keep him in bed. When the most excruciating throes had passed, he fainted in anguish, as though he were dying.

'Don't you see, my Beautiful Beast, your mother never loved you. Does that make you sad? Are you asleep?'

*
FOUR

Louise
had
lost
everything,
even
her own body which was slowly disintegrating
as the poisons of cancer continued their inexorable course.
The beautiful child who once gave her such pleasure no
longer existed for her, now that he was ugly. He shared the
lonely fate of Isabelle-Marie, who, in spite of everything,
loved him in her own way. Like Lanz, with his clothes and
and gold cane, the doll was disintegrating. Lanz was now
only a skeleton in the village cemetery where once a year
Louise left a bunch of violets. Unhappy, but also unreasonable, Louise did not believe that she deserved the same fate,
and though she no longer had faith in Patrice's beauty, nor
in her own, she still counted on her wealth and possessions.
The farms, the meadows, and the lake, everything belonged
to her. She tried to preserve herself by the magic of make-up,
for behind her blighted face still burned the fires of pride.

It was degrading to her to have such a hopelessly disfigured monster for a son. She avoided him and thought of
getting rid of him, but could not think of any reason to send
him away.

Isabelle-Marie began to regain her health. She liked to laugh and sing, now that there was no beautiful face to put her to shame. She devoted herself to the farms and spoke gently to her daughter, which had never happened before.

Louise was surprised to see her daughter put on weight and become more good-natured, but, preoccupied as she was with her efforts in front of the mirror and with the miraculously fruitful harvest promised by the fields of her immense estate, nothing really affected her. She waited for the revenue from her cherished farms.

Nothing, however, could take the place of Patrice. And in spite of the bitter tears that fell on her gaping cheek, her body already belonged to the grave.

'Patrice!'

Patrice, who had never made the effort to reflect on anything around him, had reached such depths of neglect and despair that he began for the first time to question what was happening to him. Every evening, when Louise loosened and spread her hair upon her shoulders, he automatically came to her door. Louise would leap at him in annoyance.

'Go away.'

Then he would go outside and run to the lake where he would weep without understanding, while before him was reflected the image of a young man he had never known.

'What have I done to the water?'

When he looked in his mirrors he asked, 'Why have you become so ugly? I am afraid of you.'

Isabelle-Marie tried to amuse him but he distrusted her; he was afraid of what this unnatural sister might do next. Freed from her jealousy, she now baked bread for him, made up his bed with clean sheets, and let him wander with the horses. She thought that Patrice had really forgotten whose hand had attacked him, whose fiendish nails had triumphed over him. Meanwhile, Patrice, still alive within his scarred face, daydreamed unhappily.

'Tell me, Mother, why did Uncle Patrice become so ugly
all of a sudden? One night I saw you, Mother. You told him
to put his head in the water, but the water was very hot.
Didn't you know that, Mother? Are you angry?'

Isabelle-Marie slapped her daughter. This child, who was
always shunted roughly back and forth, continued to eat her
bread. It was again dinnertime, the hour when enemies within a family pass judgment upon each other in silence. Louise
raised her diseased face and stared at her daughter with a new
gleam in her eye.

'What was that? What is your daughter saying, Isabelle?'

Isabelle-Marie blushed.

'Mother, you are not going to believe the words of a child,
are you? Anne, go outside for awhile. You can eat later on.'

But Louise grabbed the child's wrist.

'Anne, my darling, Patrice would never tell me how he
burned himself. Did you see what happened? Did you?'

The child was about to speak. Isabelle-Marie, her cheeks
blazing, her eyes protruding, answered quickly, 'Anne was
asleep.'

'No, I wasn't asleep,' the child cried. 'I was looking
through a crack in the door.'

'Tell me, my beautiful child . . .'

'I am not beautiful,' said the child gently.

'Won't you tell me? Please.'

'Be quiet, Anne.'

Isabelle-Marie clamped her fingers over the child's mouth
to keep her from talking. The child pulled away from her
and ran to Louise, who had called her a 'beautiful child.'

'Mother said to Patrice, "Lean over, you can gather the
sparks in your hand, like stars."'

'And then, my beautiful child?'

'Then he leaned over. And Mother . . . Mother . . .'

'Yes?'

'Mother pushed him into the water.'

Isabelle-Marie and Louise both turned pale. Little Anne soon forgot the horrors she had unearthed. She wanted to ask her grandmother why she had a scar on her cheek; she even wanted to stick her thumb in it.

Louise gasped, 'Don't touch my cheek.'

Frightened by this new tone of voice, the child kneeled in front of Louise.

'I'm cold,' she sobbed.

When Anne looked at her mother she felt even colder. The two women were eating each other alive, dueling with their eyes. Their souls emerged, grotesque and monstrous.

Anne pleaded, 'I want to go to bed.'

No one heard her.

'Yes, I was the one who disfigured Patrice,' Isabelle-Marie said softly.

Then, as she spoke, rebellion rose within her.

'Mother, ever since I was a child you adored Patrice because he was beautiful and hated me, the ugly one. Patrice, always Patrice! You never loved me and you never realized that your son was stupid, that he was an idiot . . . nothing but a beautiful body. Not even a man, or a child, either. Your darling Patrice never had a mind. Did you think I had no feelings just because I was ugly?'

Isabelle-Marie was choking with sobs and shaking so hard that her flesh seemed to slip from her bones. Anne looked at her, as curious as a grown woman about this tragedy which she was witnessing but not realizing that the tragedy was also her own.

'Those who saw me spurned me, even my husband. His sight was given back to him so that he could see me, and I disgusted him. But weren't you the one who made me so

104

ugly? Answer me, Mother. You condemn me, but my only crime was being alive. Because I do want to live, and breathe —in spite of my face.'

Her voice had risen to a howl and she begun to weaken, her body twisted into a degrading and futile attitude of prayer.

'Mother, I despise you because you never believed in anything but your own damnable beauty. How could anyone take pity on me when my own mother rejected me? I was jealous, too. I was dying of jealousy. Did you know that when people used to look at Patrice on the train, I wanted to die? Yes. And when the tutors came and went into ecstasies over Patrice's face, I wanted to kill him. I gave him bread that was too fresh to poison him in the night, and when I bathed him, I hoped that he would drown.'

She collapsed, limp and parched with thirst.

'Anyway, he was only an idiot.'

Louise had not spoken. Her cheek was bleeding and blood fell on her white collar. Horror dilated the pupils of her eyes. She lifted her daughter up and struck her across the shoulder.

'Leave my house, Isabelle-Marie. Go away tonight, and take your daughter with you. You hurt Patrice. But you won't hurt my land. It is mine, mine. Patrice was also mine. Get out of here.'

Isabelle-Marie raised her head, which was bathed in sweat.

'I will not leave. I love my work in the fields. I have given my life for this harvest.'

'Leave.'

Louise was crying. She waited passively for her daughter to go. Isabelle-Marie dressed Anne and before the night was over, on the same train whose passengers had admired her sleeping brother, the two of them left the farms.

Louise knew that her daughter was giving up everything and would miss the land desperately.

Isabelle-Marie, vicious and now utterly rootless, cursed

her, 'You are rotting away, Mother. Your cheek is killing you. And don't be too sure of your land . . . Soon . . .'

Anne crushed some violets in her hand as they walked to the station. She did not want to leave. She did not want to play, or even to live.

Nearly naked, with Isabelle-Marie's dogs at his side, Patrice wandered in the woods. He looked at the lake, while the dogs nestled their warm muzzles against his beautiful hands. The sun was divided into two faces, red and gold, two profiles which embraced when they met. Patrice knelt on the shore with his head in his hands and cried as a child would cry.

'What is the matter with me?'

A violent fear brought back memories of his sister, her gestures, and her words. Suddenly everything cried out to him, 'Patrice, you are an idiot.' The trees, the sun, the lake, and the birds . . .

Where did these visions come from? Isabelle cutting the bread, Isabelle sneering and, above all the other images, his mother with her black cheek.

He lay down in the sand, trying not to hear the voices which echoed within him. He was in tears; he bled tears.

'Patrice, you are an idiot,' an inward voice kept repeating, along with Louise's sickly endearments: 'My baby.'

He saw the sun in the water, but could not find his own reflection. His eyes were blinded with tears.

Then, when he finally caught sight of his wild expression, his hideous mask brutally outlined in the water, he cried out, 'How ugly I am!'

And the voice murmured, 'And an idiot, too!'

An urge to run came over him, as in the days of his fevers. He fled back to the house, his heart intoxicated, his body out of control. He was fleeing the prison of his fear, only to be caught up in the terrible rhythm of human life.

When he knocked at her door, Louise did not answer. She was lying down, disheveled, resting her cheek on a damp towel. Her forehead was pale and moist with fever. Patrice pushed the door open with his knee and penetrated the shadows that Louise had gathered around herself to welcome the approach of death.

'Leave me,' she said in a weak voice, 'I am tired; I don't want to see you.'

'Mother,' he pleaded, holding out his hands, 'why didn't you tell me?'

'Tell you what?' she asked, disagreeably.

She sat up on the edge of the bed, pulling away the towel, and with it a shred of her maimed cheek. She looked into the shadows, penetrating them with her eyes. Never again would she look at her son. Instead of drawing her closer to him, suffering had isolated her.

'Answer me,' she said. 'Don't you know that I loathe you? Yes, I detest your suffering and your ugliness. When I married your father, had I foreseen the hazards of childbirth . . .'

'Mother, why didn't you tell me that I was an idiot?'

She burst into nervous laughter.

'Patrice, did you come in here to play the clown? Do you want me to laugh? Well then, I am laughing. Listen; I am laughing at you.'

Her forced hilarity was grotesque and her cheek blazed with an even more lurid glow.

Patrice remained serious, benign, surprised.

'Is it true that I am an idiot? Why didn't you ever tell me, Mother?'

She went on laughing compulsively, carried away by this private joke, until Patrice finally threw himself at her feet, sobbing.

'Isabelle-Marie used to say that I was an idiot. She called me the Beautiful Beast.'

Louise stopped laughing. It came to her that he had only

played at innocence throughout his childhood. Animal guile, she thought to herself. Without looking at him, she pulled him off the floor and helped him to sit down. He had stopped crying. He waited, his features lined with the heavy despair of an ugly man.

Louise had just thought of a way to get rid of her unattractive son. Since he played the idiot so well, she would take him seriously and put him in an asylum.

After all, she said to herself, it's his own idea.

'What are you doing, Mother?' Patrice asked with fear in his voice.

'We are going to take a trip.'

She took a shirt out of a drawer and dressed Patrice.

'A trip, wouldn't you like that?'

With his face half-hidden in his hands, Patrice ventured to ask, 'Do you love me, Mother?'

He wanted to kiss her but she pushed him away with delicate cruelty.

In the train the passengers looked at the young man with the fire-ravaged face and the perfect body. Remembering all the long trips of his childhood, Patrice tried to lean his brow on his mother's shoulder. Louise fended him off with a malicious pinch.

The bandaged doll was ashamed; now fifty years old, she watched her ridiculous little world coming to an end. No one in this family had ever been young.

In the station people stared, not at Patrice who was beautiful, but at Patrice who was ugly.

'Is it far?' he asked.

Louise took her son by the hand. They walked toward the asylum in silence, between tall stone walls at the end of which, like a cathedral with bars, stood a dismal white refuge.

Louise tightened her grip on his hand.

*

4

Patrice was alone at the asylum and more deserted than ever, even by his thoughts. He was like a living corpse, surrounded by the life of others. He had been put away now for two years. Up until that time, he had never felt such a desperate need to think about something. Now he was always asking himself questions, the way a child does about miracles.

'Am I a mirror or am I Patrice?'

Everything in his mind was confused. He had lived for so long with mirrors, in front of mirrors, inside mirrors. All his memories were superimposed, as in a nightmare.

Once in a while his instincts would well up more strongly, but then everything would grow empty again. His understanding was at the mercy of the images that rose before him. When they fled, abruptly, he would even forget who he was. If he tried to focus on any one object, his face became hideous. Concentration twisted his features and the muscles protruded, as though revealing that he was not a man, but a beast.

His spirits sagged. His heart searched where nothing could be found. Some evenings, as he stood staring at the wall, his childhood would come back to him.

Poor Patrice had not been born a complete idiot. But his mother had done everything for him, while all he had ever done was sleep and passively exist. Louise had put words in the child's mouth, and he had never felt the need to search for them, to wrench them from his hidden soul. He became retarded, spending all his time walking and racing, and his only spiritual discovery was that of his own beauty, when he was fifteen years old.

Now it was all over. Within him there was nothing more to discover. Behind the iron bars, Patrice was cold. An urge to run obsessed him. At night, he thought of his horses or else cried out, his fists clenched beneath the sheets, 'Isabelle-Marie, give me some bread.' He could not remember why these words were so painful.

He walked with the others at the hour they all went to wash their hands, dressed in grey, each with a number on his wrist.

Why were their faces so white?

So white that he wanted to scream. Some looked from side to side, others cried into their hands or laughed hilariously. The smell of their bodies was disturbing, like the odor of corpses. And everywhere, corridors and closed doors that blocked the sun.

The day he was admitted Louise had held her son by the hand, her eyes lowered. Trembling with shame, she was no longer able to admire, as she once had, her own beauty in the touching face of her child. She refused to see the resemblance.

Find my horse—and disappear, said Patrice to himself, in a dream.

The thought made him cry.

Patrice did not like to be alone. It made him afraid. Was it not, more than anything else, the fear of having to accept his own shriveled face? Sometimes he would be found in a trance, his nails digging into his cheek. He was watched, spied upon, though he did not know it. His idiot's mind was analysed, as well as all his most intimate struggles to survive, to rise out of his private void. But he did not live; he existed. Nor did he think. Animal instinct furnished him with all the motivation necessary for his narrow existence. Often he would wake up, stricken with the dizzy terror of being suspended above himself and the rest of the world. Would a soul finally be born within him, like inspiration in a budding genius? No. Would he ever be able to live, even for a moment? No. Just long enough to desire immortality? No. Had the spirit ever once animated his heart, the heart of the Beautiful Beast? No. He had had the soul of an Adonis, but Adonis had been murdered.

He was not free. He was like someone being strangled but who still survives somewhere within himself. His eyes always shone with an intelligence that was not there. In the depths behind this false light, dark fleshy shapes ate each other alive.

He was burdened with terror—at the sight of himself.

When he was among the other patients he laughed when they laughed; he cried to taste the tears running down his cheeks. He took refuge in the security of games, in the lightning mentality of madmen, which is constantly erased and renewed in their endless waiting.

5

He had a friend, one who played his role most convincingly. Faust, a retired actor with a savage expression, held a deep fascination for him. He had hands that were always shaking, and a curly white head that was not of this world. This strange soul had also, in certain ways, the heart of a child. He was attracted by the traces of beauty in Patrice's maimed face.

In order to pay him homage, Faust imitated Patrice's expression, contorting his own face. He could create such a fantastic resemblance that Patrice feared him, the way he feared mirrors. Faust made an enthusiastic game out of everything that was asked of him.

This weird madman was obligingly crazy.

Faust leaned forward, making his nails into claws, widening his eyes like a wild animal's.

'Look,' he said, 'I am a cat.'

Patrice had only to watch closely to believe him. As Faust imitated the tortured howls and pleasures of a cat, Patrice, lost in the many scenes of his past, heard inside himself the feline laments that he had once heard in the woods. Faust wandered about his room, abandoning himself for hours to this pathetic game. Often he would be found sound asleep, striking a droll pose.

Faust could also play the clown and Patrice would play the king to please him. When it was over they would laugh together. They were their own audience, and their performance had no curtain.

Faust did not like to play dead.

'Faust,' Patrice pleaded ingenuously, 'won't you be a horse? Then I could jump on your back and we could gallop far away . . . to the other side of the forest, where there is a lake and some fish.'

Faust stood up . . . His eyelashes fluttered gently above his Mephelphelean eyes.

'But I *am* a horse. Don't you see, a magnificent steed. Ready to mount.'

Patrice clung tightly to Faust's back and cried, 'To the woods! To the woods!' They galloped around the room, carried away by this desperate game of make-believe.

'Is your lake far from here?'

'Straight ahead. You must go through the forest.'

Panting, Patrice saw the lake, and in it was his beautiful face, floating there like the dress of a drowned girl he had seen one summer night.

'Faust, there it is.'

They struck their heads against the wall. Faust fell over. Patrice held his arm.

'A beautiful lake, isn't it?'

Faust who was glowering savagely, did not answer.

With his neck extended and tears in his eyes, Faust twisted himself into the image of someone who is afraid. He pretended to hear the thunder, to feel the storm in his bones. Soon Patrice was the one who was afraid, and Faust rested, letting the illusion take effect, like an actor who has given the ultimate performance. By unleashing on someone else the dramatic passion that welled up inside him, Faust found relief.

He acted so well that Patrice believed everything; he lived through it physically. Faust would enter Patrice's room in the morning, shake hands, and then perform all day. Shaken by real tears, moved by his tragedies, Patrice would then have to humor him.

'What would you like me to play now?'

'I want you to be my mother's shoulder, just once.'

But Faust had already decided what he wanted to be.

'I am a king. You are my prince.'

'I am your prince.'

'Prince, listen to the trumpets.'

Faust was seated. Patrice remained standing by the window watching the approach of spring. A nuptial abandon reigned in the garden, and Patrice savored lily of the valley along with the smell of over-laundered linen. Unhappy springtime! . . .

'Patrice, I mean Prince, are you listening?'

'Yes,' he murmured wearily.

But he was listening to the lunatics playing below in the courtyard. Some played with marbles. One old man walked back and forth without stopping. He clutched a piece of paper to his chest.

"My treasure . . . Silence, please!'

'Do you like the trumpets, Prince? They are for you.'

Faust rose and threw open the window. He held his hand to the light and each fingertip seemed to touch the sun. The sad murmur went on outside, like the beating of a punctured drum.

'Prince! What are you thinking about?'

Patrice was bored. The king felt like crying.

Faust was pretending to be a violinist. Leaning on his bed, he ran his fingernail up and down the instrument he had conceived out of his madness.

'Listen to this. I am a great violinist.' He listened to his imaginary bow. 'What a sweet sound!'

No one else could hear his soul's music. He was alone. More alone than anyone because he understood why he was alone.

Patrice was dreaming about his mother's shoulder.

Patrice was dreaming about someone who no longer loved him.

Faust died in the month of May, while imitating a snake. Patrice leapt upon him, shrieking. He had to be held back and calmed with damp towels, for he wanted to beat his fists against the wall. Faust died like a man who has never known how to pray or to live, only to suffer. He had resigned himself to pathetic virgin pleasures. His inspired and beautiful white head, stricken down in the midst of intoxicating illusions, disappeared, and Patrice was left alone, desperately alone within himself.

Perhaps an animal deserves to be listened to when it cries. By the gods, yes, but by men?

Faust was dead. He closed the eyes of his soul when the violence of the tragedy became too much for him. His features slipped from his skin and gave way to the mask of death. And for the first time Faust stopped murmuring to himself as he slept.

6

Patrice, utterly abandoned, was not able to live at the same pace as the other idiots. One dream from his past still devoured him: My mother, her shoulder.

He had lost this security. No one cared about his sadness, not even the old man who walked back and forth across the courtyard, nor the men who had carried Faust's coffin on their shoulders. The old man was only walking for his own sake. Idiots are always searching for their souls.

Patrice was alone. He bit his lip, and was often stricken with convulsions, as on the day when his head had been plunged in the fiery waters. His muscles burned with energy and in the midst of his visions he would hold out his arms toward an empty lake.

Faust's death had grieved him deeply and Patrice went everywhere trying to find his smell, his laughter, his acts, just as instinct had once made him pursue the fragrance of his mother. Weary of never finding anything, he clawed in torment at the walls. Suddenly a spiderweb wafted down upon his still majestic arm. Patrice laid it against his cheek and fell asleep. At dawn the spider was crawling along his skin. Patrice spoke to it.

'After all, we are alike; we are stupid.'

The spider was making a star-shaped spot of blood on his arm. But what was one tiny though intricate drop, when an ocean of blood was drowning Patrice?

This purple ocean never escaped from him; it overflowed from within.

Fleeing from the others, Patrice contemplated the spider. Terrified of losing it, he kept it in one corner of the room. From the abyss inside of him, he could hear his mother's shrill voice: 'Watch out, my baby.'

Still longing for a warm shoulder, he offered his own to the spider.

'No one will hurt you,' he said.

But the spider was not content to stay there. It wanted the freedom of the walls, to excavate little shrines in its own way. One night Patrice strangled it without meaning to; the hand of this man who was still half child crushed the spider under one cold fingernail.

Now Patrice had nothing.

'I will go home to my mother. I will look for my face in the lake. Perhaps my beautiful face is still there.'

7

A woman and her little girl were walking very fast.

'The train has wings instead of wheels,' said the little girl.

Isabelle-Marie clutched the small bony hand. She spoke sharply, but the frightened child did not hear her.

'I don't like stations,' said Isabelle-Marie.

She held a lantern high in one trembling hand as they crossed the summer-scorched fields. They were approaching Louise's farms.

Isabelle-Marie shivered.

'Mother, I think your hand is sick. Let me carry the lantern for you.'

'Quiet,' snapped Isabelle-Marie.

'If you should drop it in the wheatfield, everything would burn. Don't you remember when I tried it, just for fun? I burned my leg and cried all night long.'

'No, I don't remember. You must have been very young.'

They arrived. Through the blinds, Isabelle-Marie caught sight of Louise's wretched silhouette. It was tilted, reflected in the mirror.

'Don't make any noise, Anne.'

'Grandmother will be so happy to see us!' exclaimed the child. 'She told me that I was beautiful.'

'Hush.'

The scrawny little child hopped on one foot, then on another, giggling.

'She will hug me in her arms. I won't be sad any more.'

Isabelle-Marie hid her daughter in her dress. Keeping close to the wall of the house, she peered in at her mother whose cancer was now at its most appalling stage. She was kneeling before her mirror, looking at her decayed cheek.

She was fearfully thin.

A little thinner and she would look like me, thought Isabelle-Marie.

Louise raised her hands to her gaunt brow. Once her skin had been pure and white. Now her mirror revealed a mauve face, streaked with black.

'I am cold,' sighed the little girl.

'Quiet.'

Isabelle-Marie clamped a fierce hand over her daughter's mouth, ready to hurt her if necessary. Anne had never seen such a smile on her mother's lips, a smile glowing with blood and saliva. She had smiled this way once before, when she plunged her brother's head into the boiling water.

'Why are you looking at me like that, Anne?'

Isabelle-Marie frowned, suddenly tightening her arms around her daughter, as though to crush her.

Then she lowered the lantern to her knees.

'I am cold.'

But Isabelle-Marie was still looking at her mother's image in the mirror.

'She is wasting away. I have come just in time to see her struggle for life, she who has never known how to struggle for anyone but herself.'

At that very moment Louise was thinking, I will not die; I will not die. She leaned against the window, as she had done in 'the days of her son' and cast a dismal glance over her fields and siloes that were bursting like golden bellies.

'Of course, I am rich.'

But her aged mouth was swimming in pus.

Isabelle-Marie saw her thus and condemned her, though she was no longer the same woman, no longer the mother who had mistreated her ever since she was a child, the tireless, ever-more-powerful tormentor. Anne reached out for Isabelle-Marie's guilty arm.

'Can't we go home? I am so cold.'

Isabelle-Marie smiled, a cruel and determined expression on her face.

8

Isabelle-Marie hurled the lantern into the driest sheaves of straw. She thought that it was Louise's land that she was destroying but suddenly she realized that it was God's land. Terror rose to her eyes. And shame. Everything instantly caught fire, and she stood there, weak and disenchanted, watching the mammoth bonfire.

At last she fled to join her daughter, who had run on ahead. Behind her everything began to grow purple, in a vast, apocalyptic roar.

Surprised by this glimpse of hell, Louise asked herself if it was the last agony. She cried out, suffering in every fiber of her being.

'My farms, my farms are on fire!'

But she was suffering too much to be dreaming. She put her hand on her brow. Her heavy eyelids opened on a disintegrating world. Flaming ruins shot up everywhere; she watched the red vipers in their hideous struggle for her fields.

For her it was the end of the world.

Every time a man dies, it is the end of the world and the last judgment.

'God in Heaven,' Louise prayed, 'have mercy!'

But her mirror did not answer.

Overcome by the flames, she thought she heard in the distance the derisive laughter of her daughter. Having nothing left but her bones to lose in the fire, she fainted like a dancer at the end of a ballet.

Isabelle-Marie sighed. 'It is all over. Except for me!'

Her thirst for destruction was not yet quenched. She walked faster, trembling as she went. For one moment she regretted not having given as much as she had destroyed. Weeping, she felt the need for a god, one god. The train was coming. She pushed little Anne away from her, and walked toward the tracks, her heartless soul throbbing with fear.

Escaping from the asylum, Patrice returned home.

'My mother is waiting for me. She will open the door of her room and say, "But where were you, Patrice?"'

Patrice would not answer. He would lay his head on Louise's shoulder, and the two of them would burst into tears.

He found blind, lifeless ruins.

He ran closer. 'This was my mother's room.'

He spoke to her, but she could not hear him.

He disturbed the ashes as he walked. It was a world of ashes and broken mirrors.

The lake was waiting for him in the distance.

'The lake. My beautiful face!'

He kneeled near the water. The water had grown pale.

He drank before looking at himself, and once again the sun gleamed on the nape of his neck.

Suddenly he cried, 'How ugly I am!'

Then, since he had nothing else in the world but the water, he plunged his head into the lake and sank after it, looking for the beautiful face.

It was noon.

In the blue of the sky which came after the blue of the water, the Beautiful Beast found his soul at last.

The Author

Marie-Claire Blais was born the eldest of five children in Quebec City in 1939. Shy and unpopular as a child, she very early became obsessed with the desire to write. She wrote her first poem at six, her first book at fifteen and, by the time *Mad Shadows* appeared in 1959, when she had just turned twenty, she had completed some 200 poems, four novels and twelve plays (all unpublished). But she received little encouragement. Because of financial difficulties she had to leave convent school at fifteen to become a typist and could only write at night. Also, her family objected to her work – her mother was once so horrified by one of her stories that she threw it in the fire. Finally Marie-Claire took a selection of her manuscripts to Father Levesque of Laval University. He was both astounded and impressed, but told her she must learn to discipline and simplify her style. She went home and wrote *Mad Shadows* (or, as it was called in French, *La belle bête,*) in fifteen days. Father Levesque was even more shaken when he read this manuscript, but he felt it his duty to try and get it published. He took it to the Institut Littéraire de Québec and the rest is history. *La belle bête* went through two editions in six weeks, and caused the greatest literary storm the Province of Quebec had ever known. Critics either adored or reviled Marie-Claire. Many tried to dismiss her as only a flash in the literary pan, but the volume of work she has produced since has made it clear that this was a completely false assumption. By 1960, *La belle bête* had appeared in Canada, the United States and England under the title of *Mad Shadows*. A French edition had also been published in Paris.

Since then, Miss Blais has continued to produce plays, collections of poems and novels. The same powerful themes of brooding melancholy and violence; of the lonely world of the isolated individual, have pervaded all her work. Of her novels, *Tête-blanche* was published in 1960 and *Le jour est noir* in 1962. *Une saison dans la vie d'Emmanuel* appeared in 1965 and won the Prix Médicis in 1966. It was followed by *L'insoumise* in the same year. Her two collections of poems, *Pays voilés* and *Existence* were published in 1963 and '64 respectively. Miss Blais now lives in the United States.

SELECTED NEW CANADIAN LIBRARY TITLES

Asterisks (*) denote titles of New Canadian Library Classics

McCLELLAND AND STEWART
publishers of The New Canadian Library
would like to keep you informed about
new additions to this unique series.

For a complete listing of titles and
current prices - or if you wish to be added
to our mailing list to receive future catalogues
and other new book information - write:

BOOKNEWS
McClelland and Stewart
481 University Avenue
Toronto, Canada M5G 2E9

McClelland and Stewart books are
available at all good bookstores.

Booksellers should be happy to order from our catalogues
any titles which they do not regularly stock.